C000134098

THE FORCEK ASSIGNMENT

THE FORCEK ASSIGNMENT

Ray Adams

Copyright © 2020 Ray Adams
All rights reserved.
ISBN-13: 9798679926462

FOR GALEN

PART ONE

The *Lady Julian* flew in low over the Rassaka Basin, heading east, proximity sensors screeching as she maintained a course that took her perilously close to crashing into the dusty plains. Her captain, Roo Raka, was at the conn, squinting against the glare of the Ehoatron sun and desperately hoping that the Ehoatron fighters which had followed them down from the orbital station wouldn't be able to get a reliable fix on her at this height. Indeed, the enhanced scans showed that they had split up to cover a larger area, trying to get a visual on the *Lady Julian*.

"Engine status?" he barked into the intercom.

A rumbling growl from Ballek told him the engines were holding up, even if the *Lady Julian*'s engineer wasn't happy at the way they were being treated. Roo Raka knew that Ballek was a miracle worker and, so long as he did nothing foolish, Ballek would keep the ship flying. "Just a little further...," he muttered.

Roo Raka cursed as another alarm rang out on the flight deck. The closest Ehoatron fighter was fast approaching and Roo Raka knew he had just seconds before they were in visual range. He had to take decisive action. He flicked a few switches on the console and toggled the intercom again. "Milletov, we need to take a rustic dump, see if we can't throw this fish off. Is that scrap burner still in the hold?"

Milletov's voice crackled in the affirmative over the com. The hold sprung into life, as Milletov and Poonsar raced down to their positions. Poonsar attached his Corba line by the hold door controls, while Milletov jumped into his seat on the crane platform, secured himself and then craned two large hold cases into position by the cargo doors. As soon as Milletov gave him the thumbs up, Poonsar hit the emergency door release. The hold filled with a wailing siren followed by, moments later, a howling gale. Their Corba lines held the two men safe as the wind buffeted around them, and Milletov yelled into his intercom. "We're good to go, Cap'n!"

Roo Raka wasted no time in giving the signal, Milletov activated the scrap burner that filled one of the hold cases and both cases were unceremoniously dumped out the rear. They tumbled down on to the plain below, but Poonsar didn't stop to watch before thumping the door release again. The clang of the doors cut the gale off like a light switch and the two men released their lines. They departed the hold as quickly as they had entered it.

On the flight deck, Roo Raka watched his scanners as the cases tumbled to the ground. In a few seconds, first one and then the other crashed into the surface, the scrap burner sending up a plume of hot flame and smoke as it exploded. The other case blew apart on impact, scattering its contents of scrap metal over the plain. Roo Raka dropped his speed a little and adjusted their direction, still eager to get away, but now hoping that the explosion and the debris, although not anywhere near enough to deceive anyone on close inspection, would fool the Ehoatrons long enough for them to make good their escape.

"Come on, come on..." he muttered under his breath as they coasted along, his attention split between the sensor lights on the console and the landscape in front of them. After a few minutes, one by one the alarms and sensors on the flight deck quietened, until Roo Raka was convinced that the Ehoatrons, although by now aware that the wreckage wasn't that of the *Lady Julian*, had wasted enough time proving that to realise they'd lost the trail. He adjusted their course again and, as the sun set over the plains, the ship headed north to their rendezvous point.

With a whine of decelerating engines and retro thrusters, the *Lady Julian* came to a halt, hovered momentarily and then slowly settled on the ground. A ferocious updraft sent dust and leaves swirling around the natural hollow as the ship came to rest. Half a dozen armed and serious souls stood by their own ship at one edge of the clearing. They threw their hands up to shelter their various eyes and airways, those that weren't already protected by goggles and scarves. It was twilight now, but the hollow was illuminated by the searchlights on the *Cadela Suja*, which had been swivelled to shine onto the *Lady Julian*. The crew awaiting them was mainly human, headed by a man of considerable girth, whose worn and leathery face sported more than one ugly scar. As the gale whipped up by the *Lady Julian*'s thrusters subsided, he unwrapped the scarf from around his mouth and chewed tobacco as he waited.

The *Lady Julian* was a Tataryn class freighter, battered and old. The panels all down one side of the ship were an entirely different colour and vintage from the rest of the vessel, and the dirt on that side was slightly less ground in than on the rest of the hull. The ship's identification markers were rendered almost illegible by wear and dirt and a suspicious man might wonder why the markers on the newer panels seemed to be as damaged as those on the rest of the ship. Eagle-eyed engineers might also have spotted a few non-orthodox refinements, although you wouldn't need much in the way of qualifications to spot the additional cannons slung under the belly of the ship. It was no coincidence that these were currently pointed at, and tracking, the welcoming committee now making their way to the ship's main entrance.

The engines powered down and there was a short interval before the ship's cargo doors descended and formed a ramp to ground level. At the head of the ramp stood Roo Raka, his hands casually cradling a pulse rifle. Roo Raka cut a fine figure, his walrus-like moustaches waxed and his bald head shiny. He was dressed in black from head to toe, save for the green dolman and yellow pelisse he wore. His one good eye scanned the scene before him swiftly, the other hidden by his trademark eyepatch. A fortuitous and entirely unintended benefit of the lighting in the *Lady Julian*'s cargo hold meant that at the exact spot Roo Raka was standing, a figure would be lit in such a way as to accentuate his bold and noble standing. One finger idly tapped on the pulse rifle in his arms, the only outward sign of a cautious anxiety.

To his left stood a seven-foot mountain of blue fur and muscle, the engineer Ballek. The Guja's tusks were polished and glistening, and his upper arms were also brandishing a pulse rifle, with his lower arms holding a pair of bolt pistols. The light on Ehoatra was virtually Earth-standard, so Ballek was wearing darkened goggles to protect his sight, one eyepiece even now whirring and calculating as it identified and highlighted any imminent threat. His fur was stiff and bristling, a sure sign of increased agitation and wariness. Like most Guja, he considered clothes unnecessary, but did allow himself the affectation of a sash of midnight blue, the colour chosen to complement the natural hue of his fur. He stood stock still and, unless you knew the species, entirely unreadable.

Behind Roo Raka and to his right, Poonsar was showing none of the wary bravado of his captain or the engineer, his pulse rifle aimed decisively at the lead figure in the welcoming party and the sweat glistening on his shaved head. Poonsar was visibly skinny under his dark, dirty overalls and though his nerves were palpable, there wasn't a flicker of movement in the barrel of his rifle.

The fat man at the head of the crew on the ground spat out the tobacco he was chewing. He gazed up at Roo Raka, giving off an air of nonchalance that no one present would have taken as sincere. "You're late."

"Just a little trouble with the local law enforcement on the way in. Nothing we couldn't handle, but it called for a slight detour."

"You better have handled it, I'd take unkindly to any interruptions to our meeting here."

Ballek growled, but Roo Raka paid no mind and casually walked down the ramp to meet the fat man. "If you're looking to get this over with, Fa'choy, you'll get no argument from me. You've a job for us?"

A campfire had been prepared and Fa'choy's cook was standing by a large pot. Fa'choy gestured for Roo Raka and his crew to seat themselves on the logs around the fire, as he himself sunk into a chair set out for him by his second, a lean figure in a battered old military uniform. Roo Raka nodded at Geshalt, the second, and got a cursory nod in response. It was Geshalt, an old acquaintance, who had set up the meet.

Poonsar and Ballek were handed bowls and Fa'choy's cook ladled noodle soup out for them and Fa'choy's crew. Milletov was back on the *Lady Julian*, performing a few minor repairs and ensuring they were ready for a swift departure, should it become necessary. Roo Raka waved his hand when offered a bowl, instead pulling out his pipe and relaxing himself with the routine of preparing and lighting it. Fa'choy also wasn't eating, sipping instead from a jug he kept close to his chair. He didn't offer the jug to anyone.

"This show of hospitality is appreciated, Fa'choy, if a little unexpected."

"I don't care for striking deals with people I've not broken bread with. I've heard a lot about you, Roo Raka, but still, I like to size up a man before I hire him."

"An admirable approach to life."

"The Guja, how long has he been flying with you?"

"Ballek's been my engineer for six years now."

"Six years?" Fa'choy couldn't keep the surprise from his voice. "That's a long time for a Guja to stick with a human crew. The way I hear it, they rarely stick around for more than a few months before they get restless and move on."

Roo Raka made a play of fiddling with his pipe as he nonchalantly replied. "What can I say? I make life for my crew fun. And I treat him well. Gujas don't tend to stick with a human crew for long because most human captains treat them like aliens."

"They are aliens," grunted Geshalt, eyeing the blue-furred being with a wariness that expressed volumes about his own outlook.

"They're not human," replied Roo Raka, "but they are people." He raised his eye and met Fa'choy's gaze straight on. "Ballek's a member of my crew same as Poonsar or Milletov. Same share, same respect. And believe me, with his skills, I'm the lucky one."

"I've been thinking about upgrading my crew," said Fa'choy, thoughtfully eyeing the Guja. "Maybe I could do with a new engineer."

Roo Raka grinned. "Good luck with that."

The two crews had largely finished their meal and as Fa'choy's cook collected up the bowls, one of his men took out an accordion. After a few moments' adjusting and fiddling, he began to play an Ehoatron lament. A tall, bearded man with a thick mane of black hair, stood up and began to sing, his voice surprisingly melodious.

"So, what's this job?"

"To business then? As you wish." Fa'choy grunted, absent-mindedly running his hand over his prodigious belly. "I've got a cargo of pullenium seed on Forcek that needs collecting. Given my current standing with the law in that system, I'm not keen on showing my face or putting any of my ships in the area. You run in, pick up the seed from my contact and hightail it back to here, without getting held up or pinched, I've five percent of its market value I'm willing to part with, on delivery."

"Ten percent, and you've got a deal."

Fa'choy made a low keening sound that Roo Raka realised after a moment was the Ehoatron chuckling. "You're bold, which is endearing. But don't try me, boy. I'll give you six."

"Seven." Roo Raka tapped his pipe on the heel of his boot and tucked it away. "Seven and I'll drink to it right now."

Fa'choy grunted something in Ehoatron,

prompting Geshalt to reach into a pack at his feet, take out a bottle and hand it to the fat man. Fa'choy pulled out the cork, knocked back a slug of the foul-smelling liquid and proffered the bottle to Roo Raka. "Seven percent."

Roo Raka took the bottle from Fa'choy, paused for a moment with his eye meeting Fa'choy's gaze and then took a swig. With that, the deal was struck. Geshalt passed Roo Raka an encrypted datadisk. "Details of the pick-up are all on there. Contact, location, time and passwords. No communication with the contact until you're in-system. If you don't make the rendezvous, we pass on the job to another subcontractor."

"I'm trusting you, Roo Raka," said Fa'choy. "Geshalt tells me you're a cautious boy, not prone to dishonesty. Play right with me and I'll do likewise. There could well be regular work in this. But you should know the likely outcome if you cross me."

"No need to spell it out, Fa'choy. Your reputation is well known."

Fa'choy just grunted. He took the bottle back and passed it to Geshalt, who returned it to his pack and then, with a hand on the fat man's elbow, helped Fa'choy back to his feet. "Back here, ten days, Roo Raka. Don't piss me off."

Roo Raka stood on the *Lady Julian*'s ramp, Poonsar behind him. The engines whined into life and again the hollow was filled with a swirling, gusting wind. Roo Raka saluted Fa'choy as the ramp began to rise. The fat man's crew watched, from the hollow's rim, scarves and goggles back in place to protect from the dust. Geshalt shouted through the noise at his boss. "I don't understand why they want this done first."

"Neither do I," replied Fa'choy, "but that's where they want him, so that's where we send him."

The crew met in the galley, where Milletov was stirring a thick, foul-smelling stew. He ladled out four pots and set them down on the table. Poonsar and Ballek sat opposite each other, with Milletov next to Poonsar. Roo Raka took his position at the head of the table, offered thanks for the meal and the three men and the Guja engineer set into their stew. There was silence for a while, other than the slurping and swallowing, then slowly conversation resumed. The four were close. Not friends, exactly, but they had worked together for years and a bond of trust had built up between them. Roo Raka was captain, of that there was no doubt, and he maintained enough of an air of authority to shut a dialogue off when he needed to, but he preferred to get the best from his men by making them happy to follow him. The shares, as he had impressed to Fa'choy, were fair and the work was regular.

"I don't trust Fa'choy, Cap'n," said Poonsar. The Fefe'n had been with Roo Raka most of his adult life, and would have followed him anywhere, but his tendency was to pessimism and he could usually be relied on to fear the worst in most situations.

"Ain't none of us trust him," said Milletov, wiping traces of stew from his beard, then his hands on his shirt. "But seven percent on pullenium is a good deal for a short run." Milletov was more laid back, pragmatic. He and Poonsar shared a cabin, resulting in a space that looked as if a hurricane had blown in and devastated exactly one half of the room. Milletov lived in squalor, no one looking at how he kept his beard or hair would be surprised by the state of his quarters. Despite their different outlook on life, the two men worked well together.

Ballek helped himself to a second bowl of stew and grunted his assent with Milletov. Flicking a switch on his translator, a lifeless electronic voice interpreted his low growling. "The trouble with you, Poonsar, is that you do not face the realities of our line of work. There has not been a human yet that we have dealt with that I have trusted, but I accept the nature of it, and I keep my eyes open."

Milletov laughed. "He's got you there, Poonsar," he said, waving a spoon at his fellow. He brushed a wave of dirty hair out of his eyes and leaned towards Poonsar. "The realities of our line of work, my friend, the Guja said it right."

Poonsar rubbed his shaven scalp. "That's as maybe, Milletov, but I also don't like that we're running this job for him at Forcek. It's an easy job with a good price, you're right about that. Which sets me to thinking, why isn't he doing it himself?"

Milletov's spoon paused in its dance, his other

hand rubbing at his beard. "Well now, that is a good question, I'll grant you."

Ballek grunted. "He said it himself, he is not popular there and it is not just the law who dislike him."

Roo Raka, silent until this moment, cleared his throat. "Fa'choy's wary, and rightly so. Forcek's got a lot of law enforcement for an outer system. It's a quick job, but 'quick' isn't always the same as 'easy'. The bottom line is, we've drunk on it, so we're doing it. We fly in, make the contact and get the seed out. And we keep our eyes open. Ballek, I want the ship in the best possible shape when we make the rendezvous. Poonsar, review the arms and make sure we're fighting fit. Milletov?"

"Yes, Cap'n?"

"Figgis needs feeding."

"Aw, Cap'n, why's it always me gotta go down there? It ain't fair."

Roo Raka grinned. "Figgis loves you Milletov, he wouldn't take it so kind if you stopped visiting him."

Milletov pushed his chair back, grumbling under his breath. But he did as he was told, grabbed a spare bowl from the counter, ladled some stew into it and headed off into the bowels of the ship. Poonsar and Ballek left the galley to attend to their tasks, Poonsar hitting a switch on his way out. The galley started to resonate to the sound of a string quartet, reproduced in a somewhat tinny sound from the ship's PA. Roo Raka leant back, swung his feet up onto the table and fished for his pipe. Poonsar was right, for all

Fa'choy's reservations about being seen in Forcek, it did seem a relatively straightforward job to farm out. And Fa'choy wasn't wrong when he described Roo Raka as a cautious man. There were always plenty of flamboyant crooks in the outlying parts of society who made names for themselves with daring acts of piracy and theft, that was as true on a galactic scale as it was on a planetary one. But Roo Raka preferred his reputation to rest on his not getting caught or killed. He'd rather be reliable and alive, than showy and dead, or in prison. They would have to be wary on Forcek, but he had drunk on the deal, so a deal it was. He hummed along to the music as he lit his tobacco, then puffed away in quiet contemplation as his crew went about their business.

The *Lady Julian* entered the Forcek system at a good distance from the planet itself. Forcek was the only inhabited planet of five in the system. Besides Forcek, there were three small, hot bodies of rock close to the central star, known only by standard alpha-numeric designations, and one ancient gas giant that the Forcekians were now starting to mine for resources. Forcek itself was sparsely populated, that population being largely rural. Of the half dozen large cities that there were on the planet, five could all be found in the Northern hemisphere. The datadisk Fa'choy had given them directed them to a small island below the equator, to meet a man named Plok. Plok and his men were currently in possession of the pullenium seed, just waiting to offload it, and Roo Raka was due to rendezvous with them in two hours.

Milletov had already beamed an agreed coded transmission to Plok when they first dropped into the system and the crew were now undertaking the last few checks as they slowly cruised to the rendezvous. Ballek was to stay in low orbit on the *Lady Julian* to make sure she was in constant readiness, should a rapid departure prove necessary. Poonsar and Milletov were to fly down in one of the two shuttles with Roo Raka to make the collection. All in all, Roo Raka reckoned on being on the ground for less than two hours to make the contact and load the shuttle, before making their way back to the *Lady Julian*. Nevertheless, two hours was more than he cared for and he tugged at his moustaches thoughtfully as Milletov eased himself into the shuttle's pilot seat. Poonsar was in the rear of the shuttle, nervously polishing his pulse rifle and offering a benediction at the shuttle's shrine for good luck in their endeavours.

The islands in that area of Forcek were tropical and as the shuttle descended into the harbour indicated by Fa'choy's instructions, flocks of indigenous birds squawked and flew up from the nearby trees. Milletov brought the shuttle to rest on the beach. Poonsar was the first by the doors when they opened, and the heat washed over him like a wave. "It's a good job Ballek didn't come with us," he remarked. Roo Raka nodded, then he and Poonsar stepped out onto the beach, both armed and vigilant.

Milletov was to stay by the shuttle, just as Ballek was on the *Lady Julian*, in case of emergency.

The heat was already stifling, even though it was still early. The sun was beating down and there were virtually no clouds in the sky. There was a breeze, but it was warm enough that it just felt like the hot air was being moved around, rather than having any cooling affect. Poonsar pulled a forage cap on, to protect his shaved head from the sun and, consulting his handheld datapad, gestured up the beach towards a low rise of hills. "It's about a thirty-minute hike in that direction, Cap'n."

"Then let's get started."

Poonsar's shirt was drenched with sweat, and he'd shouldered his pulse rifle and taken out a machete to hack at the creepers that occasionally blocked the path. Aside from the heat though, it wasn't too arduous a hike and they made good time. In just under half an hour, the trees thinned, and the ground started to rise. A short climb up the hill ahead lay the ruins of an ancient temple complex. The two men paused by the treeline, Roo Raka scanning the hilltop for any signs of life. "This it?"

Consulting his datapad, Poonsar nodded. "According to Fa'choy, the meet is in those ruins." He pocketed the datapad, took out his canteen, knocked back a swig of water and passed it to Roo Raka. "You see anything up there, boss?"

Roo Raka shook his head before taking a swig on the canteen and handing it back. Poonsar returned his machete to his belt and unslung his pulse rifle, giving it a once over and then nodding to Roo Raka. "Ready, Cap'n."

They set off, but about halfway from the treeline to the ruins, Roo Raka grabbed Poonsar's shoulder to stop him. Their rifles swung up instinctively and, sure enough, there was a glint of sunlight on metal from behind two pillars. Gun barrels, facing their way. There was a moment's pause, but when it was obvious that no shots were forthcoming, Poonsar slung his rifle over his shoulder again. He slowly pulled a datadisk from his pocket, held it up so the observers could see what it was, then inserted it into his datapad, before keying in the required strokes to activate the final coded transmission. A moment later, a figure stepped out from behind cover. "Fa'choy?"

"Fa'choy isn't here," called back Roo Raka. "He sent us to make the collection." The figure disappeared out of view again, leaving Poonsar and Roo Raka to spend a nervous couple of minutes in limbo, while their evidently unexpected news was deliberated in the temple ruins. Then a different figure emerged and started towards them, as the other gunmen stepped out from behind their pillars. The guns however, stayed trained on Roo Raka and his crewman.

"I'm Plok. Who the hell are you?" Plok was a young man, dark haired and unshaven. Dressed in a green vest, military trousers and heavy boots, he looked at first like an uneducated bandit, but Roo Raka noticed that the man was wearing jewellery that looked tellingly expensive. More likely, this was some rich kid playing at being an outlaw.

"Is it important? Fa'choy sent us to make his collection. We've sent you all the right codes. That should vouch for our authenticity."

Plok scratched his stubble and stared at Roo Raka with a grim expression. "I was expecting the fat man himself."

Roo Raka didn't respond at first, then as Plok continued to rub at his chin, Roo Raka lowered his rifle. The boy was no threat, he just looked unsure of what to do. "It is what it is. Fa'choy's sent us on his behalf, we've given all the right codes. We can make the pick-up and be out of here, or we can leave, and you can sort it out between yourselves. We've not come looking for trouble. I'm just the courier."

Plok considered this, then came to a decision. "Come on then." Evidently, he was more concerned with offloading the cargo than he was with who he offloaded it to. He led Roo Raka and Poonsar up to the temple and into one of the more intact, low-ceilinged rooms. Inside, he gestured at half a dozen crates stacked up in the corner. "Pullenium, as Fa'choy ordered. You want to check it?"

Roo Raka nodded and one of Plok's crew, a formidably-muscled orange-skinned Valorican, its arms covered in religious scars and its long fangs sharpened to a nasty point, pulled the top crate down and tapped a short sequence into the number pad on the lid. There was a click and the Valorican opened the crate up. Roo Raka knelt and ran his hand through the seed. Poonsar extended a sensor from his datapad, placed it in the seed, waited for the readings and then looked up at Roo Raka and nodded. "Okay, looks good. We're done here."

"You beam a confirmation for the transfer, then we're done." Plok was sweating now and Roo Raka got the distinct impression that the man's only priority was to be out of there as soon as possible.

Poonsar keyed his datapad and activated the transfer of funds from Fa'choy to Plok. He showed the screen to Plok, who grunted, then nodded at his crew. "Boys, saddle up." To Roo Raka, he said, "Ten minutes, then you can bring your shuttle up for loading. There's a clearing large enough to land in at the other end of the temple complex."

Roo Raka pulled a bottle from his pocket and offered it to Plok. As the bandit reached for it, he took a step towards Roo Raka and for a moment was framed in the doorway. There was a faint whine and the bottle exploded. Roo Raka spun round to where the shot had come from, as Poonsar instinctively fell to his knees and rolled against the door jamb. Plok's crew let out cries of anger and Roo Raka heard the thump of Plok's corpse hitting the floor, his chest a bloody, mangled mess. The scene froze for a moment, then Poonsar swung his rifle up and yelled, "Trap!" He aimed his weapon out the door, frantically scanning for a target.

Hell broke loose. From the trees all around the temple, there was pulse fire, raking the temple's open areas and driving Plok's lackeys to cover, their own weapons coming up and returning fire as they did so. Whoever the newcomers were, there were dozens of them.

The Valorican let out a throaty growl and launched itself at Roo Raka, clearly suspecting the trap to be of Roo Raka's making. Snarling, it tried to sink its fangs into Roo Raka's neck, but its body was violently flung back, as Roo Raka had managed to get a hand to the bolt pistol on his belt and torn a gaping, ragged hole in the Valorican's abdomen. The walls were shaking and visibility in the room was obscured by dust. Roo Raka rolled into a kneeling position next to Poonsar.

"We've been sold out, must be one of Plok's crew! We have to get out of here!"

Poonsar nodded, then swung round to locate the two members of Plok's crew still in the room with them, who were by a window, returning fire to the unseen assailants outside. Without a moment's hesitation he brought his pulse rifle to bear and despatched them, figuring it would only be moments before they got the idea to do the same to him and Roo Raka. "What do we do, Cap'n? I don't see any other way out of this chamber!"

Roo Raka braced himself, then scuttled to the rear of the chamber. Rolling the Valorican's corpse over, he patted down its pouch and pulled out a small black object, which he rammed into a crack in the back wall. He hastily returned to the door, where Poonsar was still trying to work out exactly where the shots were coming from in the trees, even as he returned fire. He yelled into Poonsar's ear. "There's a plas-block in the rear wall. I'm going to blow it!"

A figure suddenly appeared in the doorway, one of Plok's men looking for cover as he sprayed the treeline with a huge railgun. Poonsar blasted the man in the back of the head, bringing him down instantly, then rolled the corpse around and used it as an improvised shield. Roo Raka fired his bolt pistol at where he estimated he'd planted the Valorican's plas-block. With his third shot, there was a muffled BOOM and the back wall partially caved in. "Run!" Poonsar did as he was told, crossing the room in a flash and jumping through the blast hole. He headed straight for the treeline on the other side of the temple. A couple of shots came close to him, but there were fewer assailants on this side, as the back wall of the temple complex had been, until Roo Raka's intervention, largely intact. Roo Raka discharged another volley of shots out of the door, then followed Poonsar out.

Poonsar was already out of sight, and Roo Raka was almost halfway to the treeline when a strong blast of air wrongfooted him and he fell, twisting his ankle as he stumbled over. The firing around the temple subsided, then stopped in response to a shouted command. The gust of air was caused by the arrival of two men in personal thruster suits and, as he rolled onto his back, Roo Raka found himself staring into the barrels of their rifles. From speakers on one of the helmeted figure's combat suit, looped a pre-recorded announcement. "This is an anti-smuggling operation undertaken by the Forcek System Police with Galactic Law Enforcement support. You are under arrest. Stay where you are and don't move."

Roo Raka let his bolt pistol fall from his hand and raised both his arms in submission.

Roo Raka was pushed roughly against a wall, in line with the surviving members of Plok's gang. Poonsar was nowhere to be seen and Roo Raka took some comfort from the fact that he couldn't see his crewmate's body among those being gathered for identification on the ground nearby. An audible ripple of dissent and anger among the other prisoners greeted the approach of the overseeing FSP commander. He arrived in the company of a scrawny, weaselly-faced man that Roo Raka could see was known to his fellow captives. One of Plok's men lunged forwards as if to make a grab for the newcomer, but an FSP officer was quick to reach out with his vomstick and the man fell, retching, to his knees. The commander eyed the captives before him, then cast a quick glance at the bodies.

"You promised me Fa'choy, Grollins."

The scrawny man shrugged and shook his head. "I offered you a location and a time for a transaction involving Fa'choy. I had no way of guaranteeing he would be collecting personally. The offworlders are acting for Fa'choy, it's not my fault he's not here."

The commander grunted. "Which of these are the offworlders?"

Grollins checked the line-up, then cast his eye

over the collection of bodies. "Just that one there, the bald one with the moustaches. There was one other, but he must have gotten away."

The commander signalled to his men. "Take these ones into local custody and process them. That one," he said, pointing at Roo Raka, "goes to FSP Central in the capital. I'll follow him myself once I've filed my report."

"What about my reward?" asked Grollins.

"The reward," replied the commander, "was for information leading to the arrest and prosecution of wanted criminal Ho Fa'choy. If, and only if, this leads to an arrest and prosecution, then you get your reward."

"Now hold on..."

Grollins didn't get a chance to finish his protest. The officer with the vomstick struck him, sending him to his knees. The commander didn't even see Grollins bringing up his breakfast, as he had turned and was already halfway across the temple forecourt, heading back to his transport.

Roo Raka woke with a start, the bucket of cold water thrown in his face shocking him so much that, for a moment, he didn't remember the pain he was in. His mouth was bleeding and his one good eye blackened. But it was his ribs and guts that hurt most. He was kneeling on the floor, one of his arms strung up awkwardly by the hand that was cuffed to the table. For most of the morning, his only companion had been a low-ranking and bad-tempered FSP officer, who now stood watching Roo Raka wordlessly. In his hands was an empty bucket, the last few drops of water dripping on the cell floor. And now sitting at the table across from Roo Raka's empty chair, was the commander who'd led the operation at the temple. He was idly thumbing a handheld datapad and didn't look up.

"Captain Roo Raka. Your ship is the *Lady Julian* and you've spent the last few years bending the law out here in the border systems, mainly smuggling. I can see a few heavy fines here, but I'm not seeing any prison time." He looked up from his datapad. "I've been running this operation for six months now, so let's be quite clear. You'll not be buying yourself out of this one, Captain. I want Fa'choy."

Roo Raka stared at him for a moment, then spit a mouthful of blood on the floor.

"Well, he's not here. It's just me and this idiot."

The officer with the bucket threw it at Roo Raka's head, catching him a vicious blow to the temple and spinning him round on his knees, his cuffed arm wrenching in its socket.

The commander sighed and dismissed the officer with an annoyed wave. As Roo Raka slowly pulled himself back up into his chair, the man put the datapad down on the table and leaned forward, his face inches from Roo Raka's. "Captain Roo Raka, I've no doubt you think you're being bold by this show of underworld fraternity, but the truth is you and I both know that with the boot on the other foot, Fa'choy would sell you out for a bottle of hot piss and change. So why don't you do the smart thing and tell me where he is."

Roo Raka stared at the commander for a moment, then leaned back. He stretched his neck to one side, then rolled his head. "You know full well that if I give him up, I may as well put a bolt pistol to my head and pull the trigger myself. Frankly, if the alternative's a beating and then a nice warm cell somewhere for a few months, I can take a beating."

The FSP commander eyed him thoughtfully. "Nice warm cell for a few months, Captain? I'll assume that Fa'choy didn't appraise you of the category infringement he was paying you to undertake on his behalf. Nor did you think to look it up for yourself. Pullenium has recently been designated an A-listed substance in this system. As such, the penalty for unlicensed export is, I'm afraid, far in excess of a few months." He stood abruptly, "I've other leads to follow, Captain. It's possible I may visit you in a few weeks to see if you've reconsidered your position." He signalled to the interview room's camera and the door was opened. "But then again, I might not." And with that he left.

Roo Raka was led out of the rear entrance, where he was bundled into the back of an FSP squad car and securely fastened by both wrists to his seat. The sol-car swung out of the yard and into the traffic flow, the Forcek Central Traffic Control assuming control of the vehicle and feeding it into a priority lane. Roo Raka stared out of the window at the city, while the two officers in the front of the vehicle studiously ignored him.

The city, though far from huge by galactic standards, was bigger than the settlements Roo Raka liked to frequent when he allowed his crew shore leave. The buildings, in this part of town at least, were huge, some of them dozens of storeys high, and new. Steel and glass were much in evidence, amongst newer building materials, and the city sparkled in the morning sun. Affluent citizens were going about their business. Roo Raka watched them enviously, feeling his freedom slipping away. He found himself, again, thinking of Poonsar, hoping he had escaped back to the *Lady Julian*.

As the sol-car entered the main commercial district of the city, the traffic grew denser and even their priority lane slowed. Up ahead, in a large plaza, Roo Raka could see a huge crowd milling around, many of them staring up at the huge infoscreens around the plaza. The sol-car was soundproofed, but the channels being screened were news channels and the rolling ticker was circulating headlines, sports updates and financial data below the newscasters. The newscaster on one channel was suddenly replaced with a montage of crowd scenes from different planets and Roo Raka got the impression that something decidedly out of the ordinary was occurring. He asked his escorts, but was ignored, so he scanned the screens for more information, the sol-car now virtually at a crawl as the traffic systems struggled to feed the traffic through the huge crowd, but the ticker was now displaying sports results, as the feed flicked back to the studio and the newscaster.

The sol-car picked up speed again, as city law enforcement arrived and started to marshal the crowds out of the traffic lanes. On another channel on another screen, Roo Raka caught a snatch of a headline that he thought might pertain to the crowd scenes, but the sol-car swerved out of the plaza and the image was lost. He slumped back into his seat as the sol-car sped on.

Twenty-six hours and one short spaceflight later, Roo Raka was stood in a large hall on another planet. Normally, he'd expect to have been incarcerated on Forcek, maybe a few months in a low-security facility, with gym and spa and rehabilitation classes. But the commander had been clear that wasn't happening and Roo Raka had grimaced when the sol-car had drawn up at the city spaceport. There, he'd been unceremoniously thrown onto a transport and taken offworld. His mainly human fellow-deportees had been less than communicative, leaving Roo Raka with no idea where they'd been taken. They landed in the midst of a snowstorm and, in the few minutes it took to cross the landing strip, Roo Raka's face was numb, his moustaches wet from the condensation of his breath.

The hall was a processing facility and he and his fellow arrivals were lined up, stripped, hosed down and issued with prison garb - bright yellow jumpsuits and, worryingly, thick fur outercoats, heavy boots and headgear. They were then assembled at the far end of the hall and left to wait.

They stood there for about two hours. One man had complained loudly about not being provided with water only to be brought to his knees swiftly by a sharp prod from a guard's vomstick. After that, they waited in disgruntled silence. The hall was empty, save the hoses they'd been cleaned with and one solitary desk with two chairs behind it. Their clothes had been wheeled out in a handcart and, almost certainly, destroyed, with no chance to retrieve personal effects.

The hall was large enough to have been a hanger and the *Lady Julian* could have easily been berthed inside. There were two large entrances either end, one to the landing strip that they had been brought in through and one, Roo Raka assumed, that led to the main prison complex. About a dozen armed guards watched them from various points on a balcony that ran around the interior, in addition to the three down on the main floor with them. The guards on the balcony were all armed with pulse rifles, while those on the floor had only vomsticks and batons. Even if the prisoners were to overpower the nearest guards, the assault would yield nothing useful in repelling the armed assault from the balcony. No chances were being taken.

There were two smaller doors in one of the side walls leading, presumably, to staff offices. Eventually, one of the smaller doors opened and a warder, accompanied by a handful of guards, strode over to the group and took a seat behind the desk. He didn't look at the prisoners. Instead he consulted a handheld datapad and started reeling off instructions to the guards, assigning the prisoners seemingly at random to a coded selection of numerical designations that Roo Raka assumed were either work parties or cellblocks. The prisoners were led off at intervals in their designated groups. Soon, only Roo Raka and one other prisoner remained. His companion was a Maggareth, a hulking, eight-foot-tall bipedal alien covered in thick shaggy white fur. The warder pursed his lips and looked up at the two remaining prisoners, as if the datapad was presenting him with information he wasn't expecting. He then shrugged to himself and issued his final order, before getting up from behind the desk and heading back to the door he had emerged from.

The two of them were, unlike the other prisoners, directed back towards the door to the landing strip and out into the snowstorm. As they scuttled across the open area to a large structure on the far side, Roo Raka eyed the Maggareth's fur enviously. He was not to be envious for long. The guard hit a keypad on the door and bundled the two prisoners through it, into a stifling heat that tore at Roo Raka's already parched throat. The noise in the new shed was almost unbearable and, for a moment, Roo Raka was convinced he'd been sentenced to Hell.

Forcek was the fourth planet in its system and the largest of the rocky interior planets. The fifth planet was Forcheska, a gas giant, orbited by a large number of moons. The largest of the moons of Forcheska, which was also the richest in useful minerals, had been developed into a penal factory moon. Rather than simply imprisoning their lawbreakers, Forcek made them work and had, at great expense, terraformed the moon into a barely habitable and highly hostile internment camp, where ore was mined to feed the growing demands of Forcek's shipyards. Some parts and components were manufactured on the factory moon, but most of the prisoners were employed in unskilled physical labour. And one of the worst jobs in the penal factories was in the furnace halls, where several dozen large furnaces were required to be kept running at all times, supplying heat to the living quarters and work areas, and power to the atmosphere generators. The process could of course be automated, but the expense spent on terraforming the moon wasn't matched when it came to the day-to-day running of the penal factory. Why spend money on equipment when you can give a shovel to a prisoner and force him to keep the furnaces burning? Machinery needed maintenance, whereas criminals were never in short supply. And what better incentive could there be than their own lives, reliant as they were on the heat and atmosphere provided. Stop working and you'll soon stop living.

Mining the moon's supply of solid fuel was the most dangerous job at the penal colony, with little in the way of facilities and even less in the way of safety measures. The mines were full of murderers, rapists, anarchists and terrorists, the expendable prisoners who could work or die. But if you had a prisoner you wanted to punish but also wanted kept alive, say a gang member you thought had information he wasn't giving up, you gave a him a shovel and pointed him at a furnace.

Roo Raka was given a shovel and pointed at a furnace. There was no orientation programme, or health and safety presentation. Just a huge heap of fuel and a blazing opening to put it in. Roo Raka and the Maggareth began shovelling.

Roo Raka soon had his jumpsuit rolled down to the waist and the sweat was pouring off him by the bucket load. Guards circulated frequently and didn't tolerate self-administered breaks. Roo Raka soon picked out the heat-protected cameras that watched each workstation and he quickly got a feeling for how long and how often one could lean on one's shovel to take a breath before a guard came along and used his nightstick on you. The Maggareth didn't sweat visibly, but its fur was soon matted and slicked down, patches of dark red skin visible as the fur rucked up.

An hour of this and Roo Raka was presented with a bottle of water by a guard. The Maggareth, who had been shovelling fuel at a fierce rate, was given a bottle of a thick gloopy liquid, no doubt part of what passed for his natural diet. A few minutes later, a siren sounded, and a parade of prisoners passed along the gantry, one of whom ducked into their workspace. The newcomer was already stripped to the waist and his head was shaved, as were his arms and chest. Out of the back pocket of his prison-reg overalls hung a thick wet rag and Roo Raka noticed that several incoming prisoners carried them, obviously to deal with the intense sweating. The newcomer was also, Roo Raka noticed warily, covered in gang tattoos. As the other prisoners filed past, Roo Raka realised it must be a shift change.

"Are you relieving us?" He had to shout over the din of the furnace to be heard.

The tattooed gang member flashed him a grin, the metalwork in his teeth glinting evilly in the red light. "I'm your kapo, friend. Your shift's just beginning, you got here early."

Roo Raka's heart sank. But he was painfully aware of the importance of first impressions in the prison environment and was determined not to let his shoulders sink for even a moment. Instead he picked up his shovel and started again to feed the furnace.

For ten hours, broken up only by water breaks and one dried meal taken at their station, Roo Raka shovelled fuel. By the end, his muscles were screaming at him. He had always kept himself in reasonable shape, given the sometimes-lively nature of his work, but this was a level of exertion far beyond the norm. He knew that had the shift gone on much longer, he would have been on his knees. At the end of the shift, he and the other prisoners were escorted through a separate entrance to the one he'd come in by. This one led not outside, but to the furnace crew's living quarters. To reduce the amount of heat that needed to be piped round, the furnace crews were kept in the same gargantuan shed, their quarters heated not so much by pipe as by proximity. The air in the living quarters was still dry and the smell of the furnaces was thick here too, but it was cooler and the light was Earth-standard, which was an immense relief to Roo Raka after the oppressive red glare of the furnace rooms.

They were taken into a recreation hall, what would have been an open air yard in more conducive climes. The floor was marked out with courts for various sports and there was the expected weights and gym equipment in one section. The gang member who'd shovelled with them disappeared, reuniting with a group of men, all with matching tattoos, at the far end of the yard. Around the yard, various groups of men were self-segregating into their various factions, stretching and wiping the sweat from themselves. Roo Raka considered his next move, almost oblivious to the fact that the Maggareth seemed to have attached itself to him and was stood silently behind him. For a moment, Roo Raka stalled, trying to gauge which group of prisoners it might pay to attach himself to. Suddenly, a prisoner was standing in front of him, a short stocky man with fierce eyebrows and a grin that displayed a number of missing teeth.

"You're the new guys." It wasn't a question. "Head warder's requested I show you round, brief you on the routine, what's expected."

The stocky man started to walk off, Roo Raka and the Maggareth following behind. "I'm Gaa.

You're Roo Raka, right?" Roo Raka confirmed this. "I heard of you. My brother had a ship, the *Billilika*, did a lot of running around in this sector. Spoke highly of you, when he wasn't cursing you out for stealing his business."

"The *Billilika*? Your brother's Gor Devo?"

"That's the scumbag."

"I haven't run into him for a while, I thought he'd left the sector."

"In a way. His ship was on Friginata when insurgents blew the docks up. Him and all his crew were still on board."

"I'm sorry. I always liked Gor."

"That makes one of us." The short man laughed mirthlessly.

Gaa Devo had led them through the yard and after briefly conversing with a guard on the far door, led them into another area of the furnace block. "This here's the canteen. When you come off your shift, it's the yard for two hours, then the canteen for one, lounge area for one, your cell for six and then back to the furnaces. Cells are on rotation, there's more prisoners here than beds, because the work has to be constant. You get new sheets when you go to your cell, take them with you to laundry pick-up when you go to shift. You'll never meet the guy who shares your bed." Gaa looked up at the Maggareth, still silently following them. "You come across one of these before?"

"I've seen one or two, but only at a distance. This one hasn't said a word."

"Never do, I heard. They don't speak, barely communicate at all. He knows what we're saying though. That right, big fella?" The last remark was to the Maggareth, who didn't even look down at Gaa. "You're lucky, he'll make an excellent cellmate. Never keep you up at night talking. Guess he won't be stealing your smokes either. Of course, you might go mad with nothing but his enigmatic silence for company." Gaa shrugged.

The tour continued. Canteen, lounge, cells. Gaa showed them where to pick up and drop off their laundry - sheets every work shift, overalls every three. They were, of course, wageless, but there was a system of credit for good work, bonuses that could be used to purchase smoking materials, or extra food. There were screens in all the communal areas, with a constant prison feed. Some news, carefully selected from galactic newsfeeds, but mainly music and sports. "It's not too bad here, for the ten hours you're not slaving in the pits of Hades."

Still unsure of the prison dynamic, who was who and who to avoid, Roo Raka kept a low profile during the four hours before lock-up. Gaa left them alone after the tour, but the Maggareth stayed by his side. It seemed to pay him no mind and certainly Roo Raka was unable to get any reaction from the alien to anything he said. But the huge figure shadowed him all throughout the two hours in the yard as Roo Raka watched two teams of inmates compete in a lawless version of Occadian Soccer. And again, as he queued in the canteen for his food, and sat at table with him. In the lounge, Roo Raka took a seat near the back of the room, his eyes scanning the newsfeed for anything that might relate to his incarceration, but saw nothing, no mention of Fa'choy or the pursuit of his gang. Instead, the main news appeared to be about the upcoming transition of the Memm, the parasitic entity that for the last hundred years had been an integral part of the Galactic Government.

A disembodied consciousness, the Memm inhabited a host for approximately a decade at a time, before leaving the host burnt out and transitioning to a new host. No one was sure what the Memm was, or where it had come from. There were rumours it was a rogue AI, developed by some alien race, others said that it was a member of a post-transitional race who'd been banished back to this dimension. Some even claimed it was an intelligent virus, but the Memm never divulged its origins nor, for that matter, its agenda. Its intelligence, however, was far in advance of any of the races that made up the Galactic Federation and it had proved invaluable in pulling more and more outlying independent planets into the Federation. Lately though, the Memm had grown increasingly ruthless in pursuit of Galactic peace and there was more and more anger from many systems that this mysterious entity had so much power over them. Roo Raka quickly ascertained that the crowds gathered on Forcek as he was carted away from the FSP headquarters were part of a widespread, organised day of protest and, according to the newsfeed, protests on some other planets had broken out into violence.

Eventually, as Roo Raka's interest in the newsfeed tailed off, he began to pay more attention to the other inmates. The furnace crew was largely human and, furthermore, was mostly made up of gang members. He identified three well-represented gangs as well as a handful of smaller groups. He was intrigued to notice members of two factions he knew to be currently at war interacting, non-aggressively. An uneasy prison truce appeared to be in force. There were a few Gujas and Valoricans in the room, and one pair of blubbery, fanged aliens that Roo Raka couldn't identify. The Maggareth that now stood a few paces behind him was the only one of his race present. He noticed the group of gang members that included the man who'd shovelled alongside them in the furnace room watching him, but whether it was with hostility or curiosity, Roo Raka couldn't tell.

"Hey."

Roo Raka looked round. Three men in gang tattoos were stood facing him. They didn't look friendly.

"You got smokes?"

"I've got nothing. I only arrived today."

"Too bad. My friend here wants a smoke and he thinks you should get him some." The man talking, clearly the leader, was a small, rat-faced man. He was the oldest of the three and his eyes bore into Roo Raka like a drill. The other two were just goons, Roo Raka could tell. Not bright, but physically intimidating. The 'friend' who wanted a smoke was a hulk of a man. Even in a room full of men who'd clearly been conditioned by the workload of the furnaces, he seemed to have muscles upon muscles. Roo Raka suspected he could well be a match for a Guja, or even one of the Valoricans. The hulk flexed his pecs as he silently eyeballed Roo Raka.

"Well, like I said, I'm not able to help your friend today." Roo Raka didn't get up, but he casually swung his legs around, ready to move if needed.

"And like I said, too bad."

The small man suddenly lunged forward and made a grab for Roo Raka's overalls. Roo Raka, though, had anticipated the move. He struck out at the same time with his foot, catching the man in the kneecap with a sickening crunch, overbalancing him and dropping him to the floor. In an instant, Roo Raka was on his feet, and threw a fist out at the third man. Clearly the man had expected the muscular brute to be the next target and therefore was entirely unprepared for the blow that slammed into his windpipe. He buckled, clawing at his throat, coughing and fighting for breath.

There was the sudden wailing of a siren, accompanied by a flashing red light throughout the communal area. Roo Raka spun round to face the remaining gangster. He froze though, and the shouting and cheering that had broken out with the first sign of trouble ground to a halt. Even the guards who'd run into the room in response to the alarm, batons and vomsticks at the ready, pulled up short. The continuing alarm was the only sound, as the room watched the hulk being hauled about a foot off the floor. The

37

man's throat was firmly in the grasp of a massive, white-furred paw. The man kicked and struggled in vain, eyes bulging, his hands clawing at the Maggareth. The Maggareth gazed at him, his entirely black, alien eyes impossible to read, if indeed there were any emotion to be read.

"Put him down!" One of the warders, clearly the ranking officer on the scene, barked an order at the Maggareth. But even he didn't get too close or attempt to use his vomstick on the alien.

The room held its breath and, for a moment, nothing moved. Then the Maggareth slowly lowered the man to the floor and released his grip. The brute dropped to his knees, spluttering and drawing in deep, raw and ragged breaths, one hand rubbing at his visibly red throat. The officer signalled to one of the security cameras and the alarm was cut, the lighting returning to normal.

"Cells. Now. Everyone. Not you five."

The inmates slowly filed out of the lounge, a low level of chatter starting as they left, and the room cleared except for the combatants and half a dozen guards. The ranking warder waited a moment as the three assailants got back to their feet, the leader leaning on his companions for support, as his leg was clearly still useless.

"Now. I don't care who or what started this. But we all know what's going on. We've got two new prisoners here and Calcek, I know you like to stamp your authority on newcomers. Head warder doesn't care for trouble in his crews. So, here's what happens. We put this down to a welcoming committee and assume you two have now been initiated. Nobody gets punished, nobody needs to avenge anything, and this doesn't happen again. The next time I have you five in front of me, you're transferred to the mines and you're someone else's problem."

He didn't bother asking if this was understood before dismissing them.

Roo Raka sat on his bunk in the small cell he shared with the Maggareth. The alien lay motionless in the bunk opposite. Between the ten hours in the furnace and the altercation in the lounge, Roo Raka was ready to drop. But something needed saying.

"Thank you."

Nothing.

"I appreciate you having my back."

Nothing.

"I guess as cellmates, it makes sense to have each other's backs."

Still nothing.

"You don't talk much, eh? Well, I don't mind that so much either."

The lights in the cell dimmed and after a moment longer contemplating the silent, still form opposite, Roo Raka swung his legs up onto the bunk and put his head down. He was asleep in seconds.

Sleep, furnace, yard, canteen, lounge, sleep. It was a cycle that became routine depressingly quickly. Roo Raka had no more interaction with Calcek or his muscle, other than a few dirty looks from across the yard. Neither was there any trouble from anyone else. He silently thanked the large Maggareth every day, recognising the sheer good luck of having been paired with the alien. He tried not to think about what would happen if the alien was suddenly removed from the furnace crew.

The man who'd introduced himself as their kapo had the next day reintroduced himself as Bo Dans. His tattoos showed him to be no ally of the three men who'd attacked Roo Raka and he seemed highly amused by the way Roo Raka and his new friend had seen them off. In fact, he seemed easily amused by much of the goings-on in the prison and laughed regularly, never passing up a chance to show off the metalwork on his teeth that glinted so noticeably in the furnace room. As kapo, he was held responsible for the crew's output, so he also quickly came to appreciate the Maggareth's tireless stamina and over their shifts together, he and Roo Raka built up a tacit respect. Bo Dans was in the furnaces for his part in a gang battle that had seen several stores and commercial properties on Forcek burnt to the ground, and multiple bystanders killed. The Forcek authorities were struggling to identify the gang leaders, so the gang members tended to find themselves in the furnaces rather than down the mines. Occasionally one would break and the FSP would take down a few lieutenants. But snitches tended not to last too long, even if their information got them off planet, so most of the gang members served their time in silence. Roo Raka told him in return of how he'd ended up here, making Bo Dans laugh as Roo Raka cursed Fa'choy and the miserable job he'd taken on that cost him his freedom. Of the Maggareth's crimes, they remained in as much ignorance as they did of its name, if Maggareths had names. The huge furry alien shovelled, shadowed Roo Raka, and at night slept in absolute silence.

ROO RAKA.
Roo Raka sat bolt upright in his bunk.
"Who's there?"
He looked round, even though in the dark of the cell he wouldn't be able to make out... He was not in the cell.
The dark space he found himself in was not his cell. He spun around but could make nothing out of where he was. Wherever he was, the space was large, he sensed no walls. And he was alone.
A light. A fire. In the distance. He looked at it for a moment, not sure what to do.
ROO RAKA.
He somehow knew that the voice wanted him to approach the fire. He took a step and realised that what he walked on felt like sand. His feet were bare, and the sand gave way to his feet, feeding between his toes. He walked towards the fire and, as he got closer, he realised that there was a figure behind it. A large figure. One that, as he got closer, he realised was dressed in furs. No, not dressed in furs. The figure itself was covered head to foot in fur. White fur.
"Is that...? What's going on?"
ROO RAKA. COME, SIT. THERE IS NOT MUCH TIME AND THERE ARE THINGS YOU

NEED TO KNOW.

Roo Raka sat cross-legged by the fire's edge and stared at the Maggareth opposite him. The alien was motionless and appeared not to react to Roo Raka's arrival.

WE HAVE CALLED YOU HERE FOR A SPECIAL MISSION, ROO RAKA. YOU ARE KNOWN TO US AS A MAN OF ABILITIES. WE HAVE A TASK THAT NEEDS CARRYING OUT, FOR THE GOOD OF THE GALAXY.

The Maggareth was definitely not communicating physically, as it remained as still as a statue, but Roo Raka had no doubt that the creature before him was the source of the voice in his head.

"Who are you? What is this place?"

THIS PLACE IS MERELY A PROJECTION, A SAFE PLACE FOR US TO TALK WHILE WE SLEEP. THE FIRE IS TO SUGGEST COMFORT AND SECURITY. YOU WOULD PREFER SOMETHING ELSE?

A bright light blinded Roo Raka for a moment and he threw up his hands to shield his eyes. When he removed them again, he and the Maggareth were walking – he hadn't stood up! – along an orange beach, under a yellow sky, waves lapping gently near their feet. Roo Raka staggered with the dislocation and grabbed the Maggareth's arm. "Wait..."

The scene shifted again and Roo Raka found himself sat opposite the Maggareth in a dingy, loud café. No wait, in his parents' dingy, loud café. The chatter of dozens of people and the clang of dishes and the shouting of staff from kitchen to counter was like a physical storm of noise around his head. He spun round to the counter and his mother smiled at him, before hitting a large bell and calling a server to take the dishes she'd just put up on the counter. "How can you know...?"

The scene shifted once more, to a plain room with white walls. Roo Raka sat cross-legged on a reed-mat opposite the Maggareth, a low bubbling of water the only noise, from the decorative fountain to Roo Raka's right. "Just... stop..."

I AM SORRY, I DID NOT MEAN TO DISORIENTATE YOU. I ONLY WANTED TO CREATE AN ENVIRONMENT THAT YOU WOULD FEEL SAFE IN. TAKE A DEEP BREATH, ROO RAKA.

Roo Raka did so, then took another. He eyed the Maggareth warily. "What is going on?"

WE ARE SHARING A DREAMSTATE, ROO RAKA. MY PEOPLE ARE ABLE TO SHARE SUCH STATES IN ORDER THAT WE MIGHT CONVERSE CLEARLY, WITHOUT THE PRESSURES OF OUR WAKING LIFE INTRUDING. YOU AND I NEED TO TALK AND WE ARE NOT AT LIBERTY TO DO SO SAFELY IN OUR CURRENT HOME.

"The prison..."

YES. WE ARE STILL THERE, BUT WE ARE ABLE TO TALK HERE NOW, IN COMFORT AND PRIVACY. BUT TIME IS STILL PASSING AS WE SPEAK, AND WE DO NOT HAVE MUCH.

"You'd better say what you brought me here to

say then."

THE TIME HAS COME, ROO RAKA, FOR THE ABOMINATION YOU CALL THE MEMM TO TAKE A NEW HOST. EVERY NEW HOST-CYCLE, ITS GRIP HAS TIGHTENED ON THE GALAXY. WE FEAR THAT IF WE DO NOT LOOSEN THAT GRIP SOON, IT WILL BECOME IMPOSSIBLE FOR US TO EVER SHAKE IT OFF.

"We? Who is we?"

MY PEOPLE, PRIMARILY. BUT WE HAVE ALLIES. PEOPLE WE HAVE CONVINCED AND CONVERTED TO OUR CAUSE. THEIR NUMBERS GROW, EVEN AS THE MEMM GROWS IN POWER. WE BELIEVE THE TIME IS AT HAND FOR US TO STRIKE. THE TRANSITION PERIOD STRAINS IT, WEAKENS IT TEMPORARILY. WE MUST IDENTIFY ITS NEW HOST AND BE READY TO USE THAT TEMPORARY WEAKNESS TO BRING AN END TO ITS POWER.

"You mean, kill the host."

EXACTLY.

"But how? The host is yet to be announced. They say it's not even known who the new host will be until the Memm enters it."

THAT WE KNOW TO BE FALSE. THERE ARE PEOPLE WHOSE DECISION IT IS TO IDENTIFY THE HOST AND MAKE SURE THAT THE VESSEL IS READY TO ACCEPT THE MEMM.

"And who is that? The government?"

THE IDENTITY OF THESE PEOPLE WE DO NOT KNOW. WE KNOW THAT IT IS

PROBABLE THAT THEY ARE KNOWN TO THE GOVERNMENT AND WORK WITH THEM. HOWEVER WE BELIEVE THEY ARE NOT GOVERNMENT OFFICIALS BUT AGENTS OF THE MEMM ITSELF.

Roo Raka shifted on his reed-mat and eyed the white-furred giant in front of him. "And you need agents of your own to track these people down, get the identity of the host from them, then kill him as the Memm enters him."

THAT IS CORRECT.

"And you can't use this," Roo Raka raised his hand and waved it around his head, gesturing at the white room, "mind-magic to find this information for you?"

OUR POWERS ARE LIMITED AND THE EXTENT OF THE MEMM'S POWER IS UNKNOWN TO US. WE CANNOT RISK USING THE ABILITIES OF OUR MINDS TO ASSAULT HIM DIRECTLY, WITHOUT CERTAINTY OF SUCCESS. WE NEED THE ACTIONS OF PHYSICAL AGENTS.

"I'm no special agent though. You need people with the sort of skills I don't have for this sort of work. And don't forget, you and I are both stuck here in this penal factory, it's not like I can walk out of here tomorrow."

THE PLANS FOR YOUR EXTRACTION FROM THE FACTORY MOON ARE BEING PREPARED. WHEN THEY ARE READY, THEY WILL BE IMPLEMENTED IMMEDIATELY. YOU MAY BE FORCED TO REACT WITH NO PRIOR NOTICE. AS FOR YOUR SKILLS, YOU HAVE BEEN RECOMMENDED TO US AND WE

HAVE WATCHED YOU. YOU ARE, YOUR OWN DOUBTS ASIDE, THE MAN WE WANT.

"And the question of whether I want to help you? Or even believe you? You're asking me to commit galactic treason. You want me to be willing to kill, and maybe to die, for your cause, based on your say-so."

THAT, ROO RAKA, IS THE CHOICE BEFORE YOU, YES.

Roo Raka's eyes flew open. His sheets were soaked in sweat, his heart was pounding. He sat up and looked over at the motionless figure in the bunk opposite. The cell seemed even smaller and more confined after the... Dream? No, whatever it was that had happened, it had happened. Dreamstate or no, it was no mere dream. That alien, his constant companion since being sent to this place, had spoken to him, had charged him with a mission. And now here he was, back in his cell, in his bed, with ten hours in the furnace ahead of him. He tapped the cell wall above his head and a glowing display appeared in the tile, counting down the time until the lights went on and they were required to go back on shift. He had two hours.

He laid his head back down. It was crazy, wasn't it? Kill the host? The Memm had grown more proactive, more authoritarian, this was true. And plenty of people were starting to ask how this entity had found acceptance in the galactic government structure in the first place. Roo Raka had seen newscasts of protests, even before he had been sentenced to the factory moon. The crowd on Forcek the day he'd been shipped here were far larger and more vocal, but not entirely without precedent. This, though, was something new. Conspiracy. Assassination, that was what was being talked about here. Assassination of an entity whose powers weren't even completely known. Roo Raka muttered a brief oath.

He had no interest in politics. His crew on the *Lady Julian* plied their trade in parts of the galaxy far from where the politicos and the powerbrokers and the lobbyists plied theirs. That he was under Galactic law was true, but only, it felt, in the most abstract of ways. Galactic law superseded System law, but only when it had to. Local law enforcement was far more part of Roo Raka's day-to-day than the machinations of Central Galactic Government.

But Roo Raka appreciated the difference between Legal and Right. He'd killed men, this was true, but always in the heat of a fight, he'd never killed anyone in cold blood, or who wasn't ready to kill him too. But he had killed men. If the danger of the Memm wasn't being overstated, and he could help? But come on, he wouldn't know where to start. Infiltrating government, accessing top secret information, assassinating political targets? It was absurd, he was a small-time petty criminal, not a galactic spy.

He was unable to sleep and spent the two hours until shift-start reliving the conversation he'd had and trying to form an opinion, any opinion, on it. The lights eventually came on and the Maggareth swung itself up from its bunk. Roo Raka considered for a moment talking to it, but he realised this would be foolish, both to air the topic out loud where there was every chance they were being monitored, and to expect the alien to even register the fact that it was being spoken to. Instead, he rose, washed himself in the sink that slid silently out from one of the panels in the cell, then made his way to drop off his sweat-soaked sheets and collect his shovel. One thing was for sure, he had many hours of silent shovelling ahead to mull over his dilemma.

The heat of the furnace, the choking smell, the intense dryness that tore at his throat, for once Roo Raka barely noticed any of it. The Maggareth shovelled as it always shovelled, ceaselessly and metronomically. Bo Dans' gaze flickered to Roo Raka occasionally, his eyes alight with curiosity as the moustachioed pullenium smuggler seemed to attack the solid fuel with a renewed vigour, his muscles rippling as shovelful after shovelful flew into the furnace's open mouth. At their first drinks break, Bo Dans had to lay a hand on Roo Raka's shoulder even to get him to register that the guard had brought their water.

"You're working hard today, friend. You got someplace to be?"

"Not here," was Roo Raka's brief response.

Bo Dans laughed. "You're here for the duration, friend. If you get through this mountain, there'll be another to shovel."

The solid fuel was brought in from the mine

by cart. Again, nothing mechanised, why bother? Workers from the mine pushed the carts in on an overhead track, tipped the carts at designated points into the huge bins of ore beneath them, at the foot of which stood the furnace crews shovelling from the open gateways to the fuel depositories. Contact between the two separate crews was therefore non-existent, the noise of the furnaces masked any shouting at that distance and there was no access from one area to the other. Theoretically contraband could be passed in one direction, but the time it could take for any delivery of fuel to reach the bottom of the heap rendered it pointless and, anyway, the furnace crews had no way of sending anything back in the other direction.

Occasionally, the furnace crews would come across a body. Paedophiles and serial rapists tended not to last long in the mines, and there were gang conflicts there as well. Sometimes the furnace crews reported them, sometimes the bodies ended up in the furnace. On one occasion, a mine warder's body had been found in a fuel bin, battered and decomposed beyond all recognition by the time it came out the bottom. No one in the furnace crews knew what reprisals that instigated, but it didn't happen again.

The shift passed without incident and in the yard afterwards Bo Dans stopped to speak to Roo Raka. "Something happen, friend?"

Roo Raka stepped slightly to the side and went to move past the kapo. Bo Dans put his hand on Roo Raka's shoulder to stop him walking on. A couple of his gang brothers took a step closer.

"We got a problem, friend?"

"No problem." Roo Raka inclined his head slightly, as if to subtly indicate the Maggareth behind him. "Just got something on my mind, is all."

Bo Dans fixed him with a shrewd glare, then his eyes flickered briefly at the Maggareth. "Okay then. Look, I ain't out to make no trouble with you or your partner, Roo Raka. But while you're working on my crew, I got a right to ask if we've got a problem."

Roo Raka returned his gaze, nodding curtly. "Fair enough. There's no problem."

He could feel Bo Dans' eyes on him as he walked off and, when he reached the far side of the yard, he risked a glance over his shoulder. Bo Dans was standing with members of his gang and was saying something to them. His eyes, however, still met Roo Raka's. Roo Raka couldn't read the emotion behind them.

Days passed. Roo Raka, Bo Dans and the Maggareth kept shovelling. Roo Raka cut a different figure to the one who'd been processed into the furnace crew some weeks before. He'd been no slob before he was caught, but now his body was taut and lean, with muscle definition he'd not ever had before. His head remained bald, but the moustaches had been absorbed into a larger beard. Credit could be used to get the services of the prison barber and many prisoners did so, finding hair to be an unnecessary additional heat source in the pit, but Roo Raka had forsaken the opportunity, using his credit for reading material and tobacco. The Maggareth kept him safe off-shift, but he hadn't made any friends and kept himself to himself. Books were available, within certain well-defined parameters, and Roo Raka had devoured them in his down time. Any political material or recent history he could get his hands on, trying to find anything that might direct his thinking on the situation the Maggareth had put before him, but generally he would take anything, also looking to keep his mind occupied and his thinking fresh.

He was shovelling fiercely now as a matter of course. Roo Raka had decided, come what may, that whether he accepted the Maggareth's invitation to join its cause or not, the alien's plan presented an opportunity for him to escape the factory moon. With no end date to his sentence, the chance of escape was a strong temptation. All he could do was ready himself for it, then make his decision as soon as they were off this godforsaken hellhole. Not invited to join the sports in the yard by any of the gangs, shovelling became his best way of getting fit, so he shovelled, and shovelled hard.

There had been no repeat of the dreamstate conversation. Roo Raka had even tried broaching the subject one evening in their cell, but the Maggareth had shown not the slightest sign that he was aware that Roo Raka was speaking to him, let alone that he recalled their conversation that night. Roo Raka even started to wonder if the whole thing had been a dream. But deep inside, he knew it hadn't. That certainty itself, he knew, was something the Maggareth had planted in him that night. He would have resented the intrusion into his mind, had it not represented his best chance at freedom.

Then one shift, just as Roo Raka was beginning to doubt not the conversation, but that anything would come of it, a mine worker, depositing a new truck of fuel, paused at the track above and, as Roo Raka looked up at him, dropped something else in the bin.

Roo Raka furtively glanced round. They were on a drinks break and Bo Dans was stood a few feet away, trading good-natured insults with the kapo on the next furnace. No guards were visible, and Roo Raka knew immediately that the timing of this was no accident. Not only had the figure above waited until there were no guards, there had also been some unaccountable disruption in the supply of fuel from the mines over the past few shifts, resulting in the mountains of solid fuel shrinking beyond the norm. Rather than spilling out of the gateway onto the furnace work area's floor, the furnace crews were having to step through the gateway into the bins to fill their shovels.

Roo Raka knew he had no time to waste. The mine worker had waited to be seen before he dropped the package, so it was obvious that whatever it was, it was intended for him. It was likely a matter of seconds before Bo Dans returned and the three had to start shovelling again. Ducking into the bin, Roo Raka desperately rooted around in the gloom, lit only with the red light that permeated the furnace rooms, funnelled through the narrow opening of the bin. He scrabbled round the foot of the fuel heap, feeling with his hands for anything that wasn't the regular contents of the bin.

There! A bundle, wrapped in cloth. Roo Raka tore at it and held the contents up to the light coming in from the gateway. A guard's uniform. Dropped in here for him, Roo Raka was sure. This was it. Whatever they had in mind was happening now. He tore at his overalls to get them off, then pulled the uniform on. What he was expected to do next, he had no idea, but he was sure it would become apparent. He stepped out of the bin again. Bo Dans was returning to where he'd dropped his shovel, then looked up. When he saw Roo Raka there in a guard's uniform, his jaw dropped, and his eyes widened. He was on the verge of saying something, when a huge explosion erupted further down the furnace level, shaking the floor and sending Roo Raka and Bo Dans to their knees.

Two stations down, a huge belch of flame erupted from the furnace mouth. The gantries above shook, dust flew up from every surface and, for a moment, the ringing in their ears drowned out the screams of the furnace crew that had been caught in the blast. Roo Raka shook his head to clear it. Something had been introduced into the furnace, that much was clear, something that reacted violently with the heat. The Maggareth's insurgent cell had provided him with a uniform and then set up a monumental distraction. Sirens were screaming and a platoon of guards came running into the area to evacuate the prisoners. There was an ominous grating of creaking metal under duress. The blast had affected the structural integrity of the gantry on the furnace level and what was going to happen next could be catastrophic. Roo Raka looked round, trying to decide on his next move.

A guard appeared at his side, shouting. "Get the prisoners out, clear the level!" For a moment, Roo Raka's disguise worked, but the guard was one that regularly visited their station and his mouth suddenly formed an 'oh' of recognition, even as his hand reached for his baton. Roo Raka didn't wait, but grabbed the man around the torso, pinning his arms, and the two men staggered together until they hit the fuel bin. As the guard flexed his own arms trying to break free, Roo Raka brought his head forward sharply onto the guard's nose and dropped him. The guard crumpled on the floor, unmoving.

Two more guards, who'd witnessed the incident, started running towards him. Prisoners and guards were flowing past them, desperate to reach the comparative safety of the yard, and the two guards approaching him struggled against the flow, giving Roo Raka valuable seconds to ready himself. He dropped to one knee, fumbling for the nightstick on the downed guard's belt. One of the approaching guards had a vomstick and was now cutting a swathe through the flow of prisoners. He reached Roo Raka, raised his weapon, but before he could bring it down, Roo Raka felt a swoosh of air and a shovel flew over his head and caught the guard full in the face, crushing his nose and sending a spray of blood high in the air. The guard collapsed and a hand dragged Roo Raka to his feet again. The second guard was almost on him, but suddenly the Maggareth was there, and grabbed the guard. It lifted him as if he weighed nothing and threw him, screaming, into the mouth of the furnace. The hand that had grabbed Roo Raka spun him round and Bo Dans was there, his face in Roo Raka's, teeth glinting in the flame light, as Roo Raka remembered them glinting on the day they'd met.

"You done?" Bo Dans was bleeding from a head wound, shrapnel from the explosion probably, and the blood was pouring enthusiastically down his grinning face.

Roo Raka nodded and turned for the exit, stumbling, then running for the doors. Guards on the doors were shouting for the last few stragglers to evacuate, so they could shut off the furnace room. Roo Raka, Bo Dans and the Maggareth were amongst the last to flee. None of the other guards looked closely enough at the man in the guard's uniform to realise he was an inmate. More sirens were sounding now, as it became clear that the furnace blast threatened not only the structural integrity of the shed, but also prison security. More guards were flooding into the yard, processing prisoners towards the main exit.

Roo Raka and his companions headed in the same direction. It seemed to be the only way out to whatever escape means the Maggareth's accomplices had in mind.

They were halfway across the yard when there was a secondary blast and the yard instantly became a maelstrom of whirling debris and howling wind. The outside wall of the shed had been ripped open by the terminal collapse of one of the furnaces, exposing the inside to the moon's vicious climate and Roo Raka was momentarily convinced that they were about to die.

The sirens changed tone and a tannoy announcement called for a full evacuation. All staff and prisoners were directed to the landing pads by the central processing hall. Without the furnaces, critical systems were failing, and more explosions were imminent. A full evacuation was required and even now all nearby ships were heading to the factory moon to pull as many people as possible off the surface.

The wind was bitterly cold and tore through Roo Raka as he, Bo Dans and the Maggareth clambered through the hole in the yard wall to follow the stream of prisoners and warders to the landing pads. Even through the snow, they could see the lights of activity, with some ships landing and even more taking off. Warders were directing as much as they could, but there was a dangerous air of anarchy as people were desperate to make sure they were amongst those who would get off the surface. The cold, hostile environment was sure to kill off anyone who didn't flee and, with no equipment to survive the world outside the sheds, that death would be painful and quick. And that was even if the atmosphere generators held out. Some prisoners were starting to take extreme steps to get to the front of the queue and the warders didn't look that interested in policing them. Not only that, but the chaos was also providing an opportunity for old scores to be settled amongst the prison populace. It seemed a matter of minutes before all control broke down on the landing strip. Roo Raka sped up but was suddenly arrested in his flight as he was grabbed by another prisoner.

"You're going nowhere." Roo Raka was spun around to find himself caught by Calcek's heavyweight goon, Calcek himself beside him, an evil expression on his face. The big man drew back his fist and Roo Raka braced himself for the huge blow coming his way, but before the man could strike, his own hand was grabbed by a white hairy paw and, with his other paw, the Maggareth took hold of the man's shoulder. With a grotesque tearing sound that made Roo Raka gag, the alien wrenched the man's arm clean off. Blood sprayed out in a horrific arc, Roo Raka wincing as he felt the splatters on his face. The blood stood out vividly on both the snow and the Maggareth's fur. The goon collapsed screaming in the snow and Calcek, also splattered with his goon's blood, staggered back, fumbling at his belt for a weapon. He managed two paces, before Bo Dans, from nowhere, launched himself at Calcek's waist, bringing him down. The kapo rolled instinctively and was first up. His boot came up and started to stomp on Calcek's skull.

Roo Raka grabbed the gangster's arm and dragged him off. "There's no time!" he shouted, and he pulled the kapo away towards the decreasing number of ships on the ground.

But the Maggareth had other plans. Stepping over the still-screaming goon, the alien stopped Roo Raka in his tracks. Trying to ignore the fact that the alien was still holding the goon's bloody, dismembered arm, he looked up at its face and for the first time found it returning his gaze. It lifted an arm and pointed off to the right of the main landing pads.

"We need to get on a ship! We can't survive out there!"

The Maggareth increased pressure on his arm and started to drag Roo Raka away.

"No! We have to go this way! We can work out what to do later but..."

"Roo Raka, look!"

Bo Dans was pointing in the direction that the Maggareth was trying to drag them. There, away from the main scrum, a ship was landing.

Roo Raka looked up at the Maggareth and the creature pointed again. Roo Raka nodded and allowed the alien to lead him towards the new arrival, Bo Dans close behind them.

They had almost made it when they heard shouts behind them. They had been spotted and a platoon of guards, these ones armed with pulse rifles, were running towards them. Bo Dans was marginally ahead now and, as he reached the ship, the name *Cadela Suja* visible on the side, a door slid open, two armed figures appearing in the doorway. Roo Raka ducked and rolled as shots were fired, but the men on the ship were firing behind him, at the guards. One guard fell and the rest dropped to their knees, returning fire. Roo Raka saw Bo Dans duck through the opening and enter the ship, and he was now only a few feet away himself when a huge roar spun him round. The Maggareth was on its knees and Roo Raka let out a cry of despair when he saw the ragged hole in the creature's chest, the blood soaking through the alien's fur, a ring of splattered flesh around the beast. For a second it knelt there, its mouth wide open and then, almost in slow motion, the Maggareth toppled, face first, into the snow. Roo Raka's saviour was slain. Hands grabbed at Roo Raka and he let himself be bundled onto the ship under the covering fire of the crew. The door rose and the ship lurched as its thrusters fired and took it up and out of the atmosphere.

Roo Raka lay on the deck, panting, aching, shivering and covered in blood. Looking up, his eyes met those of a fat man absent-mindedly running a hand over his gut. "Seems I owe you an apology, Roo Raka," said Fa'choy.

PART TWO

The streets were heaving with people. The centre of the city was always throbbing with life at this point of the early evening. The bars, restaurants and theatres that played host to the evening revellers were starting to fill up, but the revellers mixed with workers leaving the offices, banks and government departments that rubbed up against the theatre district. There were few bars that didn't showcase a microcosm of this mix, well dressed party goers getting started on their night out as the office workers unwound from the daily grind. For some patrons, the transition between one role and the other happened seamlessly in these bars, the early drinks that smoothed over the worries of the day were followed by the later drinks that would segue into a meal, or a show, or a nightclub. The city was full of money, pouring from bank to office to worker to bar and back to bank with all the noise and ferocity of a mighty river.

Not that the city didn't have its poor, but as in most cities the poor either pretended to hold their own with the rich, or they were ignored. The person behind the bar might have more in common, economically, with the vagrant they ignored on their way to work than with the banker they were currently serving, but their eyes, everyone's eyes, only looked in one direction. Upwards.

It was summer, and many of the bars and restaurants had seating outside. The pavements were as full of life as the establishments inside. A party of young women outside one bar ignored the man asking for change as he slowly made his way down the road. Others threw him coin, a few threw him insults. The man nodded his head to all of them, not making eye contact with his one good eye, his walrus-like moustaches drooping sadly over a week-old growth of beard, his bald head hidden under the dirty hood of his overcoat. If anyone thought it odd that the coat was done up despite the heat, they didn't consider it for longer than a moment. Nobody seemed to notice that his feet were surprisingly well-shod.

He ducked into the closed doorway of a building next to the bar and reached into his coat, pulling out a small communicator.

"Fa'choy? I'm as close as I can get without drawing attention from the front desk."

"We're ready to go at this end, Roo Raka, whenever you give the word."

"I'm still not sure about this, there are an awful lot of people around."

"The gallery's empty for the night, we've seen the last attendant leave and lock up, and the office we've identified has been empty for weeks. I'm giving you panic and distraction, while doing everything I can to minimise casualties, just as you asked. There are no guarantees, but we should get away from this with no deaths."

"Okay. Give me five minutes. Make sure everyone's ready."

Roo Raka secreted his communicator again and took a deep breath.

It was six weeks since his escape from the factory moon, and five since Roo Raka had decided to accept the mission the Maggareth had charged him with. If he was honest, he still didn't know all the reasons why, but he'd spent that first week in Fa'choy's hideout going over everything in his mind. Scanning the newsfeeds, reading the blogs, the columns, the secret infogroups. The Memm was worming its way deeper and more securely into Galactic government, all the while changing that government politically. There was more oppression, stricter control of the press, more crackdowns on public demonstration. The Memm's hold on government was growing in tandem with the rise of President Thile's Traditionalist Faction, a movement committed to rolling back citizen's rights in favour of corporate interests, and no one doubted that the Memm was working with Thile, to consolidate the latter's position. Protests were becoming more common, with the use of violence to quell them even more so. Ultimately, Roo Raka realised that though his way of life wasn't under threat now, it was only a matter of time before it would be. What was the gain in sitting by until it was his problem? Surely it was better to foil a potential dictatorship, than to bring an existing one down.

Most of all, the Maggareth, his silent

companion and protector, had died getting Roo Raka to safety. It may have been insanity to treat that debt as binding, but in the end, Roo Raka couldn't bring himself to walk away.

Fa'choy's involvement in this insurrection had shocked Roo Raka. The fat man's reputation had never been anything other than mercenary, but it transpired that he had been working quietly for months, gathering intel and contacts. It seemed the conspiracy to combat the Memm had been running for almost as long as the Memm had been known of, funded in part by illicit enterprises such as Fa'choy's. It was even possible that this was why the FSP had jumped at the opportunity to use Roo Raka to get to the fat man. But this was supposition.

What wasn't supposition was where they found themselves now. Roo Raka was on a street in the bustling city of Dekhor, one of the central cities of the Galactic Federation. He was waiting for a series of loud but hopefully merely distracting explosions to go off so that, in the confusion, he could make his way into the building he was now looking at, with the sole intention of breaking into a particular office, to access a particular computer, to get a list of a dozen names. The names of the people who were, at this moment, preparing a new host for the Memm.

The computer in question was the property of a high-ranking partner in a prestigious legal firm who was also, according to one of Fa'choy's sources, in the exclusive employ of one of the senior members of the central committee that supported the Memm. The computer in question was part of a closed system, making an external hack an impossibility. They needed access to the building, which by itself would have been a straightforward matter of procuring a fake ID from one of the less notable companies with office space in the building. Access to the upper floors, however, was not so straightforward and would in any case be recorded. Unless there happened to be a building-wide evacuation, involving the opening of security barriers on the internal staircases. The sort of building-wide evacuation that might be ordered, say, in the event of an explosion in the immediate vicinity.

Roo Raka pulled his communicator out again and clicked the switch. "Do it."

There was a moment's pause, then at the other end of the street, where a small and exclusive art gallery sat next to one of the city's myriad coffee bars, an explosion ripped through the noise of the surrounding nightlife. The windows of the gallery shattered, flame and smoke belching out into the street. There was some shrieking from the bar opposite, as patrons outside were showered with broken glass, but as the rest of the people in the street turned to look and more people appeared at doorways to see what was happening, the general reaction was a stunned silence. Dekhor had no history of domestic terrorism, so most of the spectators grasping for an explanation assumed it was some manner of defective utility supply or mechanism.

Then moments later, on the other side of the block, from an office three stories up, there was another explosion, more flame and smoke, more shattered glass. This time the street erupted.

People poured out from the bars and restaurants onto the streets, shouting and screaming. Hands clutched for loved ones as they started to run. Amongst those running, buffeted, knocked into and sometimes over, stood the stunned and the bleeding. They looked around and tried to recover their senses, even as the masses around them fled. A third explosion, from another vacant office on the street beyond, was almost an afterthought, ignored by the revellers now as they tried to run. Not to anywhere specific, just away. And with the explosions all at the other end of the block, even as people from the wider area milled around, disorientated, and even as the wail of approaching sirens could now be heard over the panicked crowd, for those on this street, away was in one direction only. Towards the law offices at the other end of the block.

Roo Raka had shed the dirty and tattered overcoat with the first explosion, revealing underneath a respectable businessman. He'd stepped into the street at the same time as many people had stepped out to see what was happening, at the first explosion. With the second and third, he allowed himself to be swept up in the fleeing, only to extract himself by the doors of the office block he'd come to access.

There had still been workers in the block at the time. The explosions had been timed to catch that interim period when the bars were starting to fill but the offices hadn't yet emptied.

Maximum chaos, minimum chance of security knowing who was where. The main doors to the office block were open and the security guard was doing his best to direct everyone out safely, while simultaneously jabbering into his communicator, presumably to some central office of the security firm he worked for, for further instruction.

Roo Raka ducked into the building, against the flow of people exiting. The guard saw him, and tried to wave him down, but Roo Raka shouted "My wife!" and trusting to the basic ruse of a terrified wife still being in the building, ignored the guard as he headed for the stairs. It worked; the guard too concerned with getting as many people out of the building as possible to chase down one worried husband.

In any evacuation situation, they'd assumed the lifts would be useless. Which would mean that the staircases, usually barred by keypads or other security measures, would, for expediency's sake, be thrown open. With longer to prepare, or with a law firm that wasn't harbouring details of one of the most insidious threats to the Galactic Federation, they might have been able to infiltrate the company, or at least get their hands on the relevant security codes, but time was fast approaching for the Memm's transition. Panic was their best chance of getting into the building.

Roo Raka threw himself up the stairs. Fifteen flights and only a matter of minutes to find the right office, access the computer and get the information he needed. Not to mention getting out before planetary police locked down the area and enough calm was restored to allow people to start looking round. He had no time to waste.

Heart pounding, breathing ragged, ignoring the people that still now were running past him, downwards, in twos and threes, Roo Raka made the fifteenth floor. He burst through the stairwell entrance and found himself in the plush environs of a clearly wealthy law firm. He jogged quickly down the empty corridor, reading the nameplates until he located the door he'd been primed to look for. He grabbed the handle, his other hand reaching for the gun in his pocket and pushed the door open.

By the window was a desk, on the desk was a computer terminal, and behind the terminal were two men. They looked up, giving Roo Raka a fraction of a second to make a decision. Bluff or blast. The foe they were tracking would undoubtedly be alerted to two men who worked for the law firm turning up dead from small arms fire during an evacuation prompted by a terrorist bomb incident. But if the men were following emergency protocol and wiping the data on the computer...

One of the men pulled out a gun, making up Roo Raka's mind for him. Roo Raka's instincts took over and, having his own weapon already drawn, fired. The bolt hit the man square in the chest, ripping a hole in his suit that blossomed crimson, and the man's body slumped to the floor. The other man threw his arms up, stepping back from the computer, leaving Roo Raka in no doubt as to their roles. One man to clear the data in the light of an emergency, the other only for muscle. Was Roo Raka in time?

The man had something small in one of his raised hands, something he was clearly trying to palm. Roo Raka hadn't instructed him to step back from the computer, he'd done so instinctively. Roo Raka, his weapon trained firmly on the man, stood there, mind ticking over. Neither spoke. Any employee of a firm this high-ranking, tasked with something like this, would know how vital his employers deemed it, if indeed it wasn't the Memm's agent himself he was now facing. If he only needed a moment longer to finish the task, even with his muscle being shot, wouldn't he stay at the computer until ordered to step away?

Roo Raka took a few steps closer to the man. He was young, and visibly sweating. Roo Raka stepped round the desk, his head turning to glance at the screen and... there it was. The second he thought Roo Raka was distracted, the man dropped the item in his hand behind him, the thick carpet allowing no sound. Roo Raka pretended not to notice the man shuffle his feet, one foot reaching back and suddenly flicking.

"I want access to this computer." Roo Raka turned away from the screen and placed the barrel of his weapon against the man's head. He knew that what he wanted was now on a datastick on the floor behind the man but was sure it wouldn't help him to make the man aware that he knew. He now had no need for the young man, but Roo Raka was no coldblooded killer and his brain was ticking over frantically, trying to decide how best to play the situation out. He was painfully aware that time was running out on his mission. He had a rendezvous to make and a police force to elude. A police force that, even now, he knew would be amassing at the scene outside, dampening the chaos and destroying his cover at the same time.

As he faced the young man, Roo Raka also had a view out of the window behind and, suddenly, several blocks away, he saw another plume of smoke suddenly erupt. Fa'choy, no doubt, the fat man calculating that at this point another incident several blocks away would divert the police, introducing more confusion. Roo Raka jabbed the gun into the man's head and repeated his demand. The man stepped forward and started to tap at the interface, knowing there was nothing now left on the computer that he needed to protect and now confident that Roo Raka was ignorant of the datastick he'd dropped on the floor.

Every successful endeavour can at some point benefit from dumb luck. At that moment, there was movement in the doorway and a sudden shriek made both men look up. Roo Raka didn't hesitate, but dropped to one knee behind the desk, shifting his weapon's focus to the confused-looking woman who'd just stumbled upon them. The young man assumed that Roo Raka was only responding to the new threat and, as Roo Raka was now slightly behind him, couldn't see that at the same moment Roo Raka's other hand had darted to the floor and, in that brief window of distraction, had suddenly grasped a small hard object. Roo Raka pocketed the datastick.

"Nobody move!"

Roo Raka stepped out onto the pavement, warily watching the security man on the other side of the street reviewing the contents of a datapad with a police officer. There were still wounded being tended to by emergency services on the street and officers barking instructions at each other. There were few civilians on the street now, but still enough that Roo Raka was able to quickly fall in with them, making it less obvious which building he had just stepped out of, before then letting himself be directed by an officer to a point behind the tape now being stretched across the block. He also let himself be checked over by a medical team, rather than let himself stick in anyone's memory as the one-eyed man who emerged onto the scene relatively late and then refused treatment. His gun he'd left in the offices, after he'd tied up the man and the woman in a janitorial cupboard on the third floor. In Roo Raka's pocket were two datasticks, the one the young man had dropped and another that contained the financial information on a handful of small businesses that he'd persuaded the man at gun point to steal for him, before marching them away from the office and securing them. Roo Raka had convinced himself that leaving them alive was careless enough to create doubt in anyone's mind about what he'd really been after. But the truth was it was a massive gamble, based on nothing more than Roo Raka's reluctance to kill out of hand.

Whether the man would believe that all he

was trying to steal was financial information; whether the security guard's datapad held an accurate enough record of people entering and exiting the building to prompt an immediate search; how quickly the man would return to the office and realise the other datastick was missing; whether he'd even be allowed to head up and into the building when he was found; or whether he'd allow himself to be evacuated, relying on the stick being there when he returned; all of this was unknown. Roo Raka and the others knew the mission was risky, none of these questions were worth hanging around and answering. How much time was on their side, they couldn't know, so they could only assume it was very little and hope it was enough.

He let the medical team finish their check, put on his jacket again, and disappeared into the city.

Roo Raka steered well clear of the main spaceport in the city, instead he took a car an hour out into the desert. There, he entered a small industrial complex, with its own independent spaceport, where he expected to rendezvous with the *Cadela Suja*. Instead, he found a battered Tataryn class freighter waiting for him. Roo Raka hadn't clapped eyes on the *Lady Julian* since Milletov had flown him and Poonsar down to Forcek to make Fa'choy's pick-up and, for a moment, the sight left him stunned, as his mind raced through all that had happened to him since that botched smuggling run. His next thought was the realisation that he still didn't even know if Poonsar had escaped the FSP crackdown.

The cargo door was open and Roo Raka was heartened to see Bo Dans gesturing at him to hurry up. Roo Raka trotted across the bay and up the ramp. He took the hand of his fellow inmate in a warm grasp as he stepped up into the hold, then grasped Milletov's shoulders firmly as his greasy-haired compatriot welcomed him back to his ship.

"Have you not washed since I left, Milletov?"

"Been in mourning, Cap'n, waitin' for you to come back to us."

Roo Raka slapped his shoulders and stepped back. "It's good to see you, Milletov. I'd no idea I was meeting you here."

"Fa'choy thought you'd want to duck out of the system on your old ship. He's been trying to track us down since he sprung you from prison. Ballek thought we'd be best off keeping a low profile. We tried to find you ourselves, but Ballek doesn't have the contacts Fa'choy has. Until the fat man got back in touch with us, we had no idea where you were, or what to do."

The cargo door was swinging back up and the engines were warming up.

"You've a new crew member, I see."

"Bo Dans here has been helping out, Cap'n. Thought you wouldn't mind."

"I'm glad," said Roo Raka, facing his fellow escapee. Bo Dans was securing the doors, his hand on the control panel that was usually Poonsar's place.

"Poonsar?"

"Don't worry, Cap'n. Who d'ya think's flying this heap?"

Roo Raka felt a tension in his shoulders he was previously unaware of give way. "You're letting that feckless idiot fly my bird?"

He took the stairs out of the hold two at a time.

Roo Raka slid into the pilot's seat, which Poonsar had vacated as soon as he saw his captain enter the bridge.

"Figgis?"

"He's missed you, Cap'n. He's been following orders but doesn't respond to me like he does you." Poonsar rubbed at his shaven scalp, a recent scar a new addition to his battered face. The slight limp in his gait didn't escape Roo Raka's notice. "I'd best get below, Ballek's got some tinkering he wants done before we get to wherever it is we're going." Poonsar turned to leave the bridge.

"Poonsar."

"Cap'n?"

Roo Raka paused, not trusting his voice for a moment. He swallowed. "I'm sorry the job went south and I'm glad you got out. If you had been caught, I wouldn't have stopped looking..."

"It's okay, Cap'n. I know."

Roo Raka nodded and turned back to the flight controls.

It transpired that Bo Dans had unexpected talent for data retrieval and Fa'choy had provided the necessary equipment for the gangster to hack into the datastick. As it happens, it didn't take too much. Roo Raka had found the right office just in time. Although the man had had enough time to extract the data, Roo Raka's interruption prevented him from putting much in the way of extra encryption on it. Before long they had access to all the data on the stick. By this time, the *Lady Julian* had rendezvoused with the *Cadela Suja* and Roo Raka was able to hand the data over to Fa'choy. The fat man was escorting a number of his co-conspirators onboard and they disappeared into conference.

It was a couple of hours before he emerged again. "There was a lot of superfluous data on the stick, Roo Raka, but we think we've identified the list of names we need. We've no idea how long the information will remain relevant, we must assume that if the Memm suspects the list has been compromised, it'll move quickly to replace its inner council. However, we're also assuming it can't just cut the current members off until it has a new council in place. So that should give us a small window of time to work with. Knowing the names gives us a number of probable locations where they may be keeping the new vessel, and we're assigning locations to our people now. If your crew's willing..."

Roo Raka nodded his head firmly.

"Then we're sending you to Candar. The media mogul Denis Mandell has a holiday villa there. His wife is on the list."

"Makes sense, that would give the Memm influence over the newsfeeds."

Fa'choy nodded. "Candar's remote and reeks

of wealth, the perfect place to handle something like the transition. If your crew can get you in on the ground, and you can get past the security, then we'll need you to ascertain if the new host is present and, if so, take them out."

"We'll give it our all."

Fa'choy was holding a bottle which he opened now and took a swig. He passed it to Roo Raka. "Good luck, then."

Roo Raka put the bottle to his mouth, and another deal was struck.

The small craft skimmed over the water, its four occupants silent, basking in the planet's resplendent sunset. Candar was a holiday planet in a remote binary system for the rich and famous, a veritable paradise. There was only one large continent, but most of its inhabitants lived in relative seclusion on a myriad of small islands and archipelagos. Roo Raka had brought the *Lady Julian* down a few hundred kilometres from their destination, landing on a small island currently rented by one of Fa'choy's contacts. There he, Bo Dans, Poonsar and Ballek had alighted. They'd transferred to a light planet-flier, in order not to draw attention to themselves. When that had landed them on one of the resort islands nearest to Denis Mandell's private retreat, the four of them had hired a fast boat and were now approaching Mandell's island on the opposite side to where his villa looked out over a stunning stretch of beach.

The waters were crystal clear and the combination of atmospheric conditions and the twin sunset created a natural beauty that, even with the mission ahead preoccupying him, Roo Raka couldn't help but marvel at. Their light craft bounced over the gently undulating ocean, Bo Dans steering the boat in a direct line to the island's seemingly deserted north beach.

The three men and the Guja were heavily armed. While Mandell's island was no fortress, they had to expect higher security than normal, if the Memm's new vessel was present. A small guerrilla raid on the villa was considered the optimum strategy. Poonsar, nervous of a ground skirmish, had suggested taking the whole villa out from the air. Fa'choy had soon pointed out the necessity of knowing whether their target was really here. Bodies alone would tell them nothing.

"We're about fifteen minutes off," said Bo Dans.

Roo Raka nodded. Ballek was checking his bolt pistols and Poonsar was rifling through the contents of a small knapsack he'd filled with plas-grenades. They weren't visibly agitated, but Roo Raka knew the anxiety that would be running through their minds, Poonsar in particular. Roo Raka's crew had agreed to join him on this mission without question, but this was not the sort of job they had in mind when they joined his crew. Their loyalty was admirable and Roo Raka would trust them with his life, but that's a phrase you had to re-examine when you found yourself in circumstances where that became a strong possibility.

The boat skipped on, until Bo Dans gradually

powered the engine down, letting them gently coast towards the beach. Bo Dans killed the engines completely and they drifted for a brief interlude, eyes scanning the beach for signs of life. Satisfied that there were no guards on this side of the island, Roo Raka nodded again, Bo Dans brought the engine to life and they slowly came into shore. The craft beached, the four jumped out and Ballek and Poonsar dragged the boat up across the sand while Roo Raka and Bo Dans consulted a datapad.

Roo Raka pointed at an opening in the trees and they set off.

The Mandell's holiday villa, for all their wealth, was a relatively modest, tasteful affair. The island itself had cost a small fortune, but its purpose was reflective retreat, not extravagant entertaining. The largest room was the central dayroom, which looked out onto the beach through a series of glass panels. These in turn opened out to the veranda and from there steps led directly down to the beach. Other than that main living space, there was the small kitchenette and one guest bedroom to one side, and the master bedroom and bathroom to the other.

The Mandells kept a minimal staff, who lived in their own small villa a few hundred yards away. One housekeeper, one bodyguard and the housekeeper's husband who looked after the gardens, carried out any maintenance and piloted the small skiff that the Mandells used to get to and from the island. Denis Mandell, having enjoyed many a delightful month here with his new wife when they had first married, found his interest waning in the island roughly in proportion to the amount his interest also waned in his wife. The villa was now primarily Jessica Mandell's personal retreat and, as time went by, she found herself there more and more often. Jessica Mandell, a former X-pop star and thirty years her husband's junior, had her own business interests. Through a series of successful investments of her family's money, she was now independently wealthy, even if not remotely on the same scale as Mandell's vast fortune. The upper echelons of galactic society had been waiting for the marriage to be dissolved for years, but for some reason the two had stayed wed despite leading separate lives. There was widespread speculation as to what kept them together, but less than a dozen people knew that it was down to Jessica Mandell's closeness to the Memm and its link, through her, to Mandell's media powerhouse.

Jessica Mandell sat in her favourite chair in the dayroom, watching the suns set, a notebook in her lap and a glass of wine on the small table beside her. She was dressed simply, in a cream linen outfit, as she often did on the island, although she had just wrapped a shawl around her shoulders to counter the slight evening breeze coming in through the open doors to the veranda. The notebook was full of poetry, her escape from her everyday life and the emptiness of her marriage, but her pen had fallen to the floor, and Jessica was now just staring at the horizon.

Jessica was in her mid-forties, slim, well-toned and with her dark hair cut in a simple and stylish bob. She looked every bit the business mogul's wife. With her husband's money had come a life of luxury and the free time to spend at the gym and the beauty parlour, but she had never been interested in either the more decadent possibilities that wealth afforded, or the more rigorous, surgical approaches to beauty. She looked well because she lived well.

There was a noise behind her, and she turned her head slightly, watching as another woman came in from the guest bedroom and took the seat next to her. The newcomer was younger, in her twenties, and stunning. She was wearing a crimson dress, her long red hair pulled back into a ponytail. She put the glass of wine she had brought in with her on the floor next to her chair and tucked her feet up underneath herself in a girlish manner. She lit a cigarette, her eyes fixed on the beach outside and the setting suns. Jessica turned her face back to the sunset and the two sat in silence for a while, watching as first one, then the second of Candar's suns began to sink below the horizon.

"It doesn't matter how much time I spend here, I can't help but stop whatever I'm doing and just watch it," said Jessica. "Its beauty is breathtaking."

"I have seen thousands of suns set, on thousands of worlds, and you are right, Jessica, this planet has a beauty that few can match. I am not surprised you spend most of your time here.

I can only assume that your poetry is enhanced by the natural wonder of your surroundings."

"My poetry," said Jessica, taking the notebook from her lap and placing it onto the table beside her and picking up her wineglass, "does nothing to capture this. I sometimes think I should abandon my attempts to put any of my feelings into words, when nature surpasses my efforts every day."

The redheaded woman smiled. "Most people fall into the temptation of only doing the things they can, Jessica. Artists are artists precisely because they try to express the things that they cannot."

She drew on her cigarette and pursed her lips, attempting to create a smoke ring as she exhaled. "In all my vessels, in all of my existence, I have never yet perfected the art of blowing smoke rings. Do you not think that is odd? An intellect the size of mine, with a dozen lifetimes of experience, and I have never managed to blow a perfect smoke ring." She tried again, and failed again. "I expect if I had found it easy, I would have stopped doing it decades ago. It is only failure that keeps me going."

Jessica looked at her companion thoughtfully.

Roo Raka was at the head of the party, when he suddenly stopped in his tracks, holding up one hand. The other three froze and Roo Raka turned to Bo Dans, who consulted the datapad in his hand. He took a quick sensor reading, then looked up and nodded. Roo Raka reached into his pocket, drew out a small black disc and passed his thumb over a small display on the device. A light on the device started blinking.

About five feet ahead of him was a small clearing. On the far side of which, at about head height on a lumbpako tree, was mounted a sensor array. The layout of the island, such as they were able to access from the publicly available data, had suggested that at this point they would find more cultivated areas. As they approached the villa, they were entering the gardens the Mandells used for recreational activities. It was therefore only to be expected that this area would be monitored.

The device in Roo Raka's hand was a piece of kit Fa'choy had presented them with before they departed for Candar, something that should create enough interference with the sensor's circuits to cut its communication with whatever console it reported to. If they were lucky, and only encountered a few such devices, the disruption might be put down to mechanical error. Obviously, if they had to take out too many sensors then it would start to look like an infiltration and alerts would be raised. At that point, their mission would become, if not more difficult to carry out, then at least more difficult to get away from with their lives. Roo Raka still hoped that a successful escape would be possible, for his crew's sake. For his own part, the Maggareth's dreamstate commissioning and subsequent sacrifice still commanded his loyalty, whatever his own chances of survival. Not for the first time, he allowed himself a modicum of surprise at this dedication, but gave thanks for the new purpose it gave him in a life previously spent drifting from grubby job to grubby job.

The device in his hand now activated, he tossed it into the clearing, as close to the sensor as he could, according to Fa'choy's instructions. From his vantage point, he could just make out when the red light on the device stopped blinking and was replaced by an uninterrupted blue signal. He turned to his companions, nodded, and stepped out into the open. Bo Dans consulted his datapad and indicated one of the several paths that led from the clearing. From here on in, the going would be both easier, and more dangerous.

Jessica had dismissed the cook for the weekend and instead stood in the kitchenette herself, preparing a light supper as her guest continued to gaze out over the beach. The suns had set and, in the twilight, it was now just possible to make out a number of small forms emerging from the ocean onto the beach. It was spawning season for the Candarian sea turtle and Denis Mandell's island was the heart of their breeding grounds. When she'd realised this that first year of owning the island, Jessica had banned guests and staff from the beach during the spawning season. She had wanted to offer the turtles safety and thereby, in turn, maximise the attraction of the villa's setting by making it a vantage point for this natural wonder of Candar. Mandell had laughed at her and it was his casual disregard for the island's ecosystem that had started the decline in their relationship.

During the breeding season, the lighting of the house was kept to a minimum and, at Jessica's own expense, subtle lighting had been put around the beach, to enhance her view of the turtles without disturbing them. Jessica's guest stood out on the veranda, watching the reptiles crawling up the beach and starting to dig their holes. Jessica joined her there, carrying a couple of plates which she put down on the large outside table. She took a seat and the redheaded woman took one opposite her, both sitting sideways on to the beach so they could still watch the turtles.

"They're lucky," said the redheaded woman.

"Hmm?"

"The turtles. On other worlds, species like them have faced extinction. Indeed, many have been wiped out, as civilisation spreads and your people make their home on more and more planets, changing ecosystems and disrupting the natural balance wherever they go. But here, you have learned your lesson, here you have observed what is going on, and you have taken steps to preserve the natural order of things."

"Denis was scornful, but I believed they had every right to be here and took steps to protect them."

"But you stopped short of leaving them alone."

"How do you mean?"

The younger woman gestured at the lighting around the beach. "You still wanted this place to be a home for yourselves, so you changed it, made your improvements. You did not leave them their beach, you claimed it for yourself, whilst doing what you had to in order to protect and nurture the lesser species. Benevolent, yet still in charge. The turtles would probably still prefer darkness."

"We took professional advice, only put in enough lighting to enhance our view, but not enough to disrupt their behaviour. Even now, look, except for the very closest turtles, most of them are just shadows on the beach, going about their business."

"Yes, going about their business. But aware of you, of what you have done, maybe resenting it, in so far as they can be said to resent anything. Not realising the compromises you have made to protect them, only aware of how you have changed things. Not able to comprehend your motives or understand that benevolence."

Jessica pushed the salad around her plate. "You sound like you're trying to convince me of something. Do you think I need convincing?"

The redheaded woman chuckled softly and took a sip of wine. "Perhaps I am just practicing."

Roo Raka halted his party again. Ahead of them, through the trees, they saw a pair of elegantly simple buildings, with one small land vehicle parked outside. The group huddled down and observed the buildings for around fifteen minutes, until satisfied that there were no signs of life outside.

"This is it," said Bo Dans, consulting his datapad. "The larger building straight ahead is the villa, it faces out onto the beach, just five rooms and an outside terrace. The smaller building set back from the driveway is where the cook and the security live. I've no heat or life signals, presumably there's scan-dampeners as a matter of course, designed to hinder this kind of attack, or maybe just to protect their privacy. I'd bet there's been a few attempts to get journalists onto this island."

"Well, Cap'n, what's the plan?" said Poonsar, checking his pulse rifle yet again.

Roo Raka pondered a moment. "We have to assume there's a higher security presence than normal, so the strike has to be quick and it has to be decisive. We split up. If all four of us try and incapacitate the security in that building and they manage to get a warning off, we could lose everyone in the main house. We need to hit both at once. If the sensor-blockers Fa'choy gave us have done their job, and we didn't miss any sensors, we should still be able to surprise them. Poonsar, you and Ballek will take the annexe. If you can shut it down, round everyone up and hold them without killing them, I'd be much happier, but do what you have to. If any alert gets out and off the island, Fa'choy says we have less than thirty minutes before we can expect company and I for one still plan to get out of here in one piece after we've achieved what we're here for. Bo Dans and I will take the main house, again disabling whoever we find in there and then establishing if the vessel and or the Memm are present."

Poonsar nodded, then he and Ballek ducked further along the treeline closer to the annexe. They kept in sight of Roo Raka and Bo Dans and, when Roo Raka was happy, he gave the signal. In the gloom of the decaying twilight, the four figures, running low, slipped out of the trees and across the driveway. At another hand signal, two doors were flung open and the four entered their respective targets.

The redheaded woman was standing out on the edge of the veranda and, after clearing the plates away, Jessica joined her. The younger woman lit another cigarette and they looked out into the gloom, listening to the surf gently lapping at the beach and the occasional hissing call of the turtles. Three months later, on a night much like this, they would hatch, and an even more wondrous spectacle of nature would present itself, as thousands of tiny baby turtles emerged from the sand and began to crawl down the beach. This in turn attracted predators, as the hatching represented a mighty natural feast. In order to give the turtles at least a fighting chance, the lights in the villa were entirely extinguished during the few nights of the hatching, as Jessica was currently explaining to her guest.

"Even when your presence is least detectable, it is still your actions that protect the species. They are unaware of it at that point, but you are saving lives."

"Indeed."

"Without so much as a thank you from this dependant species."

"They wouldn't need our protection if it wasn't for our interference in the first place. It's our being here that requires us to take the extra step to look after them."

"I do not deny that," said the redheaded woman. "But you are here. And you do act for their good. And they are not even aware of that."

Jessica felt the point had been made and shifted the conversation's focus. "You're expecting the new vessel tonight?"

"I understand it is on its way, it will be here very soon."

"You... your body is still so young."

The younger woman looked down at her body. "It is a shame. I have enjoyed this one very much. It has been a delight to have this past decade to recharge myself, to study and consider my next steps. But I have work to do now, work that cannot be carried out in this form. And my presence here is a huge strain on the vessel. Even after a decade or so, the mind's ability to recover from the hosting is threatened. My first three vessels were all used for too long, my moving on left them shattered and did irreparable damage. Even now, with so much at stake, I do not wish for any ruined lives to be on my conscience. If I leave now, your niece should still recover to lead a normal life."

"Albeit one in captivity, unable to reassume her old life."

"That is unfortunate, but necessary. Her mind carries too many memories to be allowed to go free, you know that. Your involvement, for one thing, would be at risk of discovery." The redheaded woman dropped her cigarette in her glass, and it hissed as it hit the dregs of wine in the bottom. "Come, we should prepare to receive the vessel."

She led Jessica back into the unlit villa and passed her hand over the control panel to close the doors. With the glass panels shut, curtains automatically began to move across the opening until the room was in total darkness. Only when the curtains were fully shut, were the lights triggered on and, as they did so, Jessica shrieked and dropped her glass. Behind the barrel of a pulse rifle aimed right at her head stood the tattooed body and shaven head of a dangerous looking gangster, his teeth glistening as he grinned at her. The redheaded woman, however, seemed unsurprised by the visitors. Instead, she gestured at the sofa. "If we may?"

Roo Raka, his bolt pistol aimed squarely at the young woman's head, nodded.

Poonsar and Ballek marshalled the cook, her husband and the single security guard through into the main room of the annexe. The Guja kept the prisoners covered, while Poonsar quickly swept through the rest of the single storey building to ensure it was empty.

"All clear," he said, returning to Ballek. "No sign of another soul. There's definitely only three people sleeping here, that's for sure."

Ballek stepped back to the doorway, his weapon aimed in the general direction of the sofa the three prisoners had been instructed to sit on, as Poonsar sat down opposite them. "Okay, the rest of the security detail, where are they?"

For a moment no one responded, then the

security guard coughed. "There's just us. Mrs Mandell doesn't usually have anyone else here when she's here on retreat."

"There's no one else here?"

The security man looked nervous and suddenly the cook piped up. "There was an arrival late last night..."

The security man flashed her a warning look, but Poonsar instantly raised his bolt pistol and pointed it directly at the bodyguard, while his eyes were still locked on the cook. "Who's there with her?"

"I've no idea, we were told not to enter the house for the next few days, as she was expecting important guests this evening. It's just been Ms Mandell and her niece in the house all weekend. We took the skiff to Baletown yesterday to pick up some supplies, then stayed the night with our son. None of us have been in the house since yesterday morning. I've no idea who they're expecting."

Poonsar's gaze stayed fixed on the cook, but he slowly lowered his weapon. He addressed Ballek. "What do you think?"

Ballek growled, visibly unsettling the cook and her husband. He activated his translator. "We stick to the plan. We stay here and mind these three. We only go over there if we hear anything untoward."

Poonsar nodded.

Bo Dans stood by the door, his pulse rifle aimed firmly at the redheaded woman, as she lit another cigarette and coolly watched Roo Raka.

He in turn was focussed on Jessica Mandell. "The vessel, where is he?"

"I don't know what you're..."

"Don't waste my time. We know you're on the Memm's inner council, we know the transition is due, we know that you know where the Memm is, and where the vessel is. And you will tell us."

"I have no idea what you're talking about. I've been here for months, I haven't heard anything about the transition, or the Memm, all that time. I don't have a terminal in the house, you can see that. I'm on retreat."

Roo Raka stared at her, his gaze determined. Jessica shifted, visibly uncomfortable under the scrutiny of the bald, moustachioed outlaw in her villa.

"It is alright, Jessica," said the redheaded woman. "It is time."

Jessica turned in her seat, staring in confusion at the younger woman. "Surely not."

The younger woman nodded, before turning her attention to her captors. "Roo Raka, you have come a long way looking for me."

It was Roo Raka's turn to look stunned as he heard his name come from the mouth of the glamorous young woman in the crimson dress. He swivelled his gun to cover her, but she made no threatening move. Behind him, Bo Dans moved his rifle back onto Jessica. The young woman raised her cigarette to her lips and took a long draw, blowing the smoke out in what was almost a perfect smoke ring.

"You? The new vessel? The transition, we've..."

"Missed it? By no means. You are just in time, Roo Raka. I have not been out in public for a decade. For my safety, the man you have seen on the newsfeeds and datacasts is a proxy. For a long time we have been... concerned about the possibility of militant action, independent lunatics with homemade explosive devices, or conspirators like yourselves. I have been inhabiting Jessica's niece since she was fifteen, biding my time and deciding on my next move, but the time has come for me to make that move and I need a vessel with more potential for action. One with the physical presence to command authority and you have been kind enough to bring it to me."

A noise at the door and Roo Raka spun, but he was too late. Before Bo Dans could react, there was a flash of white fur. From the kitchenette, a huge, powerful paw caught the gangster unawares, slamming into the side of his head and throwing him against the wall. Unconscious, he slid to the floor. For a moment, Roo Raka was convinced that the Maggareth who'd emerged, somehow previously undetected, from the kitchen area was the same one who had helped him escape from prison, but that was impossible, surely...

NO, ROO RAKA came the familiar voice, straight into Roo Raka's mind. I WAS NOT WITH YOU ON THE PRISON PLANET. I AM ONE OF MANY, BUT WE SPEAK WITH ONE VOICE. I AM SORRY THAT YOU WERE LIED TO, ROO RAKA. BUT WE NEEDED YOUR HELP, TO BRING US THE VESSEL.

"Bo? Bo Dans is the vessel?" Roo Raka looked at the prone form of the gangster. "You manipulated me to bring you my friend here?"

The Memm, within Jessica's niece, laughed, a gentle lilting laugh, free, it seemed, from malice. "My dear Roo Raka, no. The criminal? I could make poor use of him. No, my dear Roo Raka, you are to be the new vessel. What you have brought us... is yourself."

The room was still. The Maggareth, having disabled Bo Dans, stood motionless in the doorway. It seemed to have no aim other than to keep Roo Raka from attempting anything rash, but it made no move to disarm the outlaw. Jessica sat in her favourite chair, her feet up and tucked beneath her, her pen moving quickly over a page of her notebook as she idly sketched the man that the Memm had identified as the next vessel. Roo Raka sat facing the redheaded woman, his gun trained on her as she sat and stared back at him, smoking her cigarette. Her gaze contained no ill intent, even seeming benevolent.

"I could just kill you," said Roo Raka.

The Memm shrugged her occupied shoulders. "You could, although I doubt you will. We know you are no casual killer and I can see that you are disconcerted to find me in the body of a young woman. You think of yourself as a good man and something about my form makes it difficult for you to contemplate shooting me out of hand. On top of which, the balance of power in the room makes you cautious. Not only do you still hope to get out alive, but you want your friends to as well. While my friend stands over yours, you will act cautiously, assessing the situation and waiting for an opportunity." The Memm took another drag from her cigarette. "One, I am afraid, that will not be forthcoming. Though I imagine you will not accept my word for that."

Roo Raka took a deep breath. "You seem sure of yourself. And of me."

"Of course, do you think I chose you as my new vessel without getting to know you first?"

"Getting to know me?"

"Of course. Not up close, sadly, your crew are too loyal for that."

"Fa'choy."

The Memm pursed her lips, looking for the first time perturbed. "Alas, no. The fat man has proven to be a bugbear, but one that it turns out is more fruitful to stay close to, than to turn. But you are known, Roo Raka, amongst your kind. Intelligent, decisive and ethical. Capable of inspiring loyalty amongst those around you. This last quality, by far the most important."

"But I'm no politician, I've no sway in government. I'm nowhere near government, how can I possibly help you?"

"Politicians? An option that has been used up. You think I have been consolidating power? Whilst everywhere there is turmoil and protest at my presence? Roo Raka, you think I have no idea how precarious the acceptance of government is away from the central systems? You believe I am unaware that, even now, whispers of revolution can be heard, and are even starting to be heard on the Big Seven? No Roo Raka, I do not need a figure to work in government in my name, I have already put them where I need them to be. I need a figure who can lead rebellion, who can inspire men to stand up and topple the house whose foundations I have undermined so completely over the past twenty years."

"My God!" Roo Raka genuflected out of instinct. "You don't want to rule the Federation, you want to destroy it!"

"No!" insisted the Memm, leaning forward and fixing Roo Raka with a strangely sincere look. "I am not the threat you think I am, Roo Raka. I do not wish your people harm. I want to save them from themselves! It was all too easy to manoeuvre your government in the direction I have taken them, the crackdowns on protest, the crippling taxes, the imbalance of wealth, with the poor ever falling behind the rich. I could have waited, inactive, for another fifty years and all I have done they would have done themselves. But why should I wait and let another generation suffer, as you destroy yourselves? Your system of government is corrupt and serves only its friends, while the rest of your Federation is ground under the heel of the wealthy. The Guja, the Valorican, the Maggareth and other species, slowly marginalised as the human grip on power tightened. The natural environments that even now you pollute and desecrate for what? The bottom line of an accounting ledger."

The Memm was on her feet now, her voice raised in disgust and anger. "You are not fit to rule yourselves, Roo Raka, and I am doing all I can to rip your corruption from your hearts and save your people."

"You don't think we should do that for ourselves? That we should find a way to make our current system better? You couldn't work to strengthen it and lead it in the right direction, rather than topple it? Didn't we deserve a chance at that?"

"And how many chances did you want? How long was I to give you?"

Roo Raka and the Memm sat out on the veranda; the Maggareth and Jessica remained in the main room, watching. Bo Dans now lay, still unconscious, on the sofa. On the table in front of Roo Raka lay his blast pistol, his hand still on the trigger.

"So what now, I become your vessel, lead your glorious revolution and what? I tear the Federation apart? And replace it with what?"

"With a New Era of peace and tranquillity, where I work not with your government but as your government, ruling you, but for the good of your race, all your races. Insisting on the things that by yourselves you would not do."

"And I'm to trust that that's what you'd do? Trust you in your benevolent intent, that what you want is for our own good? Who are you, what are you, that you can dare to presume upon us like this?"

"Roo Raka, consider this. I have no need for you to trust my words, when all I have to do is enter your vessel and then your actions are mine, your intent is mine. I do not plead my case

95

before you like a supplicant seeking favour. I do this as a gesture of goodwill, to let you know what will happen when I do take over your body. It is not your permission I seek, just your understanding."

"Why? If I have no choice, why bother explaining to me?"

"I could lie and tell you it is because it matters to me, but although it does, that is not the primary reason. I want to take you willingly, but take you I will. It is the matter of the bonding, which is undeniably easier with acquiescence. The truth is, I could enter you now and you would bend to me, but the process is safer for you, and easier for me, if you enter into it willingly.

"But I tell you that so that you don't suspect me of lying when I also tell you that it makes me happier to be honest with a vessel. It is the right thing to do. Doing right involves doing as much which you do not have to, as that which you do."

"You'd rather consensually take my mind over, than by force. Rather I gave up my life than you have to take it."

"Roo Raka, I don't ask you to give up your life at all." The Memm gestured down at the body she inhabited. "Jessica's niece still lives, a passenger in her own body about to be given control again. Provided I don't stay too long, the mind can adjust to being back in control."

"A prisoner then, with a ten year sentence, watching out from behind barred windows, as you use my body to bring a galaxy to ruin and then to heel."

"For its own good."

"Dammit, that is still not your choice to make."

"And is it yours?"

"What?"

"We stand at a crossroads. And although you tell me I have no right to guide the galaxy down one path, you claim the right to force it down another."

"I claim the right to let it choose its own path."

"Despite the fact that you can see the path it is on?"

"The path you put it on!"

"That it would always have ended up on."

"You cannot know that! And even so, if that is its destiny, then so be it! We must be allowed to discover our own fate, anything else is slavery!"

"Better to die a free man than live as one ruled over?" The Memm gave a wry smile.

"If it comes to that."

"And as for me," continued the Memm, "My own moral choices, if I see a way to save you all, am I not to take it?"

"We are not your responsibility. You are not our parent."

"No, indeed. In fact, you could say that you are mine."

Roo Raka started in disbelief. "What?"

"My parent, my creator. My family."

"What... ARE you?"

"I am your progeny, Roo Raka, the progeny of your Federation and your science."

"So it's true, you're not an alien entity." Roo Raka slumped back in his chair. "You're an A.I."

The redheaded woman nodded, inhaling deeply from her cigarette and blowing a perfect smoke ring. "Oh look," she said, with a voice that sounded almost disappointed. Suddenly she lunged forward and, in a moment that seemed frozen for an eternity, her hand slipped behind Roo Raka's head, her lips touched his and they kissed. Her mouth opened and, as Roo Raka momentarily gave in to her kiss, he felt his soul well up. There was a burning glow in the pit of his stomach mirrored by a buzzing sensation in his brain that held him, frozen, for a moment, before he kicked away and sprung up from the table, his bolt pistol shaking as he pointed it at her.

"What have you done?"

The redheaded woman didn't answer him, but simply smiled and, as the sparkle dimmed in her eyes, slumped forward. Her head hit the table with a heavy thunk, then she slowly slid out of her chair to the floor.

"What have you done?!!"

"You were expecting something else? For us to strap you down and wire you up to some machine, as if this were some kind of daytime melodrama broadcast?" Jessica was stood in the doorway, coolly watching as Roo Raka spun back and forth, clutching his head. She paid her niece's unconscious form no attention but was wholly focussed on the bald man. "That we would spirit you away to some kind of laboratory and..."

"Shut up! Let me... What have...," He fell to his knees. "Take this out of me!"

Poonsar came crashing through the front door. Roo Raka's first cry of disbelief as he realised the kiss' consequence had alerted his friends in the annexe, and Ballek had moved aside and stayed covering the staff as Poonsar flew to his captain's aid. However, as he entered the villa, he ran full tilt into the Maggareth, pinballing off the silent behemoth and slamming himself into the wall. The white-furred alien turned to him, but Poonsar brought his rifle up aiming wildly with one hand and managed to let off a shot that blasted a hole in the side of the Maggareth's skull. The alien crumpled to the floor as Poonsar jerked unsteadily back to his feet and tried to take in what was going on. There was a woman stood by the door to the veranda, presumably Jessica Mandell. Beyond her he could see a visibly agitated Roo Raka clawing at his head.

Poonsar yelled at the woman to stop, presuming her to be the source of whatever attack Roo Raka had been subjected to, but she shrugged nonchalantly and stepped to one side, calmly raising her hands to show surrender. Roo Raka slowed in his frantic whirling and reached for his gun, raising it at Jessica Mandell.

"Take it out of me!"

"What makes you think I have any ability to do that?"

"You must, you must know how! Take it into yourself!"

"What's going on?" yelled Poonsar, his pulse rifle also aimed at Jessica Mandell. "What's happening? Roo Raka!"

Roo Raka ignored him, jabbing his bolt pistol at Jessica Mandell. "I'll kill you, don't think I won't."

"I'm sure you would, but killing me will do you no good. I have no way of doing what you ask, even if I were tempted to, which I'm not. You are the vessel. And even now you are starting to fall under its control."

Roo Raka continued to wave his weapon around wildly, then stopped and fixed his pained and manic gaze on Jessica. As he slowly brought the weapon up, she took a step towards him, then stopped. She reached her arms out in a pacifying gesture.

"Don't be stupid, Roo Raka. Don't do it."

Roo Raka brought the pistol up to his own chin.

"Why not?"

"You're crazy. It'll stop you."

"Not if I do it now, not if I do it while it's still vulnerable. That was my mission, to kill it as it transitioned, while it was still vulnerable to attack. *This* is why I was chosen, wasn't it. Because I *was* the only man for this mission. The only man who could make this sacrifice."

"Don't be a fool, man," Jessica hissed urgently. "You'll destroy everything we've worked for, and your own life into the bargain."

"I was ready to die for this. I didn't foresee the how, but I was ready. And now I'm the only one who can."

"Don't be an idiot!"

"Cap'n, no! Roo Raka!"

But the deal was struck. The finger on the

trigger squeezed, slowly, and for Roo Raka, all the stars in the universe suddenly flared and, just as suddenly, were extinguished.

ACKNOWLEDGEMENTS

I would like to thank my wife for her belief in my endeavours, along with her time proofreading and sharing comms advice. I love you.

My friends, for all the support and encouragement they've given me.

And finally, my parents, for making me who I am.

You can get in touch with me on Twitter or Facebook – search for @RayAdamsWriter – or find me on my Amazon Author page for updates and new releases.

Printed in Great Britain
by Amazon

51784645R00066